EE

Hannah ... down at her daughter

Joe was so busy admiring her skill as a mother, he didn't get out of her way fast enough.

Their bodies brushed. She tilted her face up to his. Their glances met, held, and it was all Joe could do to keep from taking her into his arms, lowering his mouth to hers. He knew that kissing her now would be out of line. The last thing he wanted to do was take advantage of her.

Pushing his own desire aside, Joe stepped back. He wished the situation were different, he were different. Because if he were a stay-in-one-place kind of guy he wouldn't hesitate to make a move, to see if this simmering attraction led anywhere. But he wasn't in the market for a wife and kid. And she wasn't the kind of woman looking to have a fleeting affair. It was best, then, that they stay friends.

And only friends.

Dear Reader,

We all want to belong, never more so than in our own families. Unfortunately, that doesn't always happen. Sometimes it is an act of fate that separates us from our loved ones. Other times it is a choice or a differing point of view.

Hannah Callahan wants a child and a family of her own. With no husband on the horizon, she decides to adopt a baby girl from Taiwan. Her father wants her to wait and marry and have a family the old-fashioned way. When Hannah refuses, a rift is created between them that seems unbridgeable.

Joe Daugherty was orphaned at age eight. He went to live with relatives, and never quite fit in. He could, however, *briefly* blend in with strangers.

Destiny brings Joe to Summit, Texas, for the spring and summer. He is researching a travel guide, and will soon be leaving. So when Hannah Callahan catches his eye, he ignores his desire. Until the day she needs him to accompany her to Taipei to meet and adopt her new daughter. Joe agrees to go, but only on condition that he not become involved in any of the family stuff. Family is not his forte.

Hannah concedes, but baby Isabella Zhu Ming Callahan has other ideas, right from the start. A cuter matchmaker could not be found. But could she make their love last…?

I hope you enjoy reading this book as much as I enjoyed writing it.

And, as always, best wishes,

Cathy Gillen Thacker

Cathy Gillen Thacker
HANNAH'S BABY

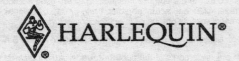

HARLEQUIN®

TORONTO • NEW YORK • LONDON
AMSTERDAM • PARIS • SYDNEY • HAMBURG
STOCKHOLM • ATHENS • TOKYO • MILAN • MADRID
PRAGUE • WARSAW • BUDAPEST • AUCKLAND

ISBN-13: 978-0-373-75222-5
ISBN-10: 0-373-75222-9

HANNAH'S BABY

www.eHarlequin.com

Printed in U.S.A.

Chapter One

Hannah Callahan stood on the porch of her childhood home, savoring the cool breeze of a perfect summer morning, watching dawn streak across the vast mountains. She had grown up in Summit, Texas, and although she had spent most of her post-college years living out of a suitcase in hotels all over the world, she was glad to leave those nomad days behind her. Glad to be starting a new chapter of her life.

A dark-green Land Rover made its way up the quiet residential street.

Hannah acknowledged the driver and wrestled her suitcase down the broad wooden steps of the prairie-style home.

Thirty-five-year-old Joe Daugherty left the motor running and met her halfway up the sidewalk. He was dressed in loose fitting trousers and a vibrant striped shirt that brought out the evergreen hue of his eyes. As always, the sheer size of his rugged six-foot-three frame dwarfed her considerably smaller body.

Hannah shifted her gaze from his broad shoulders, trying not to notice how petite she felt in his presence. She and Joe had met five months earlier. He'd come into the store, and the two of them had hit it off immediately. She'd been instantly and undeniably attracted to the sexy adventurer. He had seemed similarly interested. Had she not been so ready to settle down, and had he planned to stay in the area for more than the six months it took to research and write his book, maybe they would have gotten together. But Hannah was not interested in beginning an affair that would only have to end, so they'd relegated each other to the category of casual friend, nothing more. The fact he was going on this trip with her was a fluke, the kind of favor not likely to be repeated. She needed to remember that.

The emotion simmering inside her this morning had nothing to do with the arresting features of his masculine face, or the way the short strands of his hair gleamed against the suntanned hue of his skin. Nor did it have anything to do with the amount of time she was going to be spending with Joe Daugherty over the next week. Her racing pulse was caused by the continuing tension between her and the only family she had left. Anticipation of the events to come…

Oblivious to her tumultuous thoughts, Joe slipped his strong hand beneath hers to grip the handle on her wheeled twenty-six-inch suitcase. "This all the luggage you've got?"

Hannah nodded around the sudden lump in her throat and clasped the red canvas carryall of important papers and travel necessities closer to her body. "I just need to stop by the Mercantile and say goodbye to my dad." Try one last time to talk some sense into him.

Joe fit her suitcase next to his and shut the tailgate. "No problem." He slid behind the wheel while she jumped in to ride shotgun. He looked over his shoulder as he backed out of the drive. "We've got plenty of time."

But not enough to change her dad's mind. Hannah swallowed, beset by nerves once again. "Thanks for going with me."

Joe shrugged and flashed her a sexy half smile. "Hey. It's

not every day somebody offers me an all expense paid trip to Taiwan."

"Seriously—"

"Seriously." He sent her a brief telling look that spoke volumes about his inherently understanding nature. "You need somebody to accompany you who has a current passport and no fear of the complexities of international travel. Someone who knows that particular region of Asia, not to mention the language, and is footloose and fancy-free enough to be able to drop everything and go once you got the word it was time."

Stipulations that had narrowed the field of possible travel companions considerably. Glad he was not reading anything else into the invitation she had issued him, Hannah relaxed and settled back in her seat. "Ah, the virtues of being an adventure-loving travel writer," she teased.

Joe braked for an armadillo taking his time about crossing the road. As he waited, he grinned at her. "Versus the virtues of being a marketing whiz turned entrepreneur?"

His praise made her flush. Pretending her self-consciousness had nothing to do with him, Hannah wrinkled her nose. "You can't really call me an entrepreneur since the business I'm going to run—*if* I can ever get my dad to retire—has been in the family since Summit was founded in 1847." Since then the mountain town had gone from an isolated but beautiful trading post for ranchers and settlers to a popular getaway and tourist attraction.

The armadillo finally hit the berm. Hands clasping the wheel, Joe drove on. "The changes you want to make are good ones."

He was one of the few people who had seen Hannah's plans to turn around the slowly diminishing family business. Hannah caught a whiff of cinnamon roll as they passed the bakery. "Tell that to my dad."

"I have, a time or two." Joe pressed his lips together ruefully. "Not that he's inclined to listen to an East Coast city slicker like me."

Hannah fidgeted when they stopped at a red light. She was so ready to get to Taipei and begin her new life it was ridiculous. "You grew up in Texas."

"For the first ten years of my life—" Joe waved at a prominent rancher in a pickup truck "—but I went to school in Connecticut."

While she respected Joe's Ivy League credentials, it was the inherently respectful, compassionate way he treated everyone who crossed his path that she admired. Had he intended to stay in the beautiful Trans-Pecos area of West Texas, she might have considered seeing if the two of them could be more than friends.

Unfortunately, she knew it would never happen. He was as much a vagabond at heart as she had once been. For reasons, she suspected, that were just as elusive and privately devastating as her own.

Her mother's death and her father's recent heart attack had made her face the fact that time to address old hurts—or at the very least come to terms with them—was running out. If she wanted to heal the rift between her and her dad, the way her mother had always wanted, it had to be done soon. Whether her dad cooperated or not!

Aware the silence between them had stretched on for too long, Hannah shifted her attention back to Joe and asked casually, "When will you be done with your book?" Last spring, he'd rented a cabin just outside town and used it as a home base for his research on southwest Texas.

"It's essentially done now. I just want to take one more trip to Big Bend, to check out a couple of the hotels I missed on my earlier visits, write the magazine articles I'm going to use to promote the book, and then I'm off to Australia to start my next project."

"So you'll be leaving…?"

"Texas? Right after Labor Day."

Which meant, Hannah thought sadly, she'd rarely if ever see Joe again.

In another three weeks, he'd no longer be stopping by the Mercantile to chat up the tourists shopping there about their favorite haunts in this part of Texas. He'd no longer be teasing her, or making polite conversation with her father. Or stopping by to see if she wanted to grab some lunch at one of the cafés in town, along with whomever else their age he could round up.

Joe turned onto Main Street. The county courthouse and police station sat across from the parklike grounds of the town square, taking one whole block. Farther down, brick buildings some two hundred years old sported colorful awnings over picture windows. In the past few years, restaurants that catered to tourists and natives alike had sprung up here and there, adding to the length of the wide boulevard in the center of town. But it was the imposing Callahan Mercantile & Feed that gave Summit the Old West ambience tourists loved to photograph.

Built shortly after Texas achieved statehood, the sprawling general store still bore the original log-cabin exterior. Improvements had been made over the years, but the wooden rocking chairs scattered across the covered porch that fronted the building still beckoned a person to linger, even after purchases were made.

Joe eased his SUV into a parking space in front of the store. "Any chance the day's pastries have arrived yet?"

Hannah nodded. "My dad stops by the bakery personally every morning to pick them up before he comes in. Help yourself to whatever is there. I'll go find Dad."

Gus was in back, as she figured he would be.

At seventy, he was still a handsome man with expressive brown eyes the same shade as hers. In the two years since her mother's death, his thick straight hair had turned completely white. Gus Callahan had never been an easy man. He was set in his ways. Opinionated. He had a strong sense of right and wrong and had never been known to yield to anyone. Including Hannah.

A lump formed in her throat. Wondering when she would ever stop longing for his approval, she managed to choke out, "Dad?"

He looked up from the account statements he was sorting through.

"I'm leaving," she said wishing, once again, for a miracle.

Gus scowled and set down the stack of billing notices. He looked her square in the eye and said flatly, "It's still not too late to change your mind."

IT WAS NOT JOE'S INTENTION to eavesdrop. Never mind get personally involved in a family dispute that was none of his business. But Hannah's sigh of dismay rang through the silence of the Mercantile, catching his attention.

"Dad." Her voice sounded thick with tears, in a way it never did with anyone else. *"Please."*

Gus stormed out into the grocery aisles, either not noticing or not caring that Joe was there to witness the familial contretemps. Jaw set, he marched over to the card table in the corner where a large stainless steel percolator that had seen better days was set up. He picked up a disposable cup and held it underneath the pour spout. "I'm not going to pretend this is a good idea, Hannah." Gus glared at her over the rim of his cup. "You want a baby? There are better ways to go about getting one."

She sniffled. "It's not that easy."

"The hell it's not!" He quaffed his coffee the same way he would a shot of whiskey. "You've got cowboys and businessmen lined up from here to Austin, ready and willing to marry you."

She threw up her hands, angry now. "I don't love them!"

Gus lifted his scraggly white brow. "How do you know what *could be* when you won't even date them?" he demanded.

Hannah's jaw set, in much the same fashion as her irascible father's. "I'm not going to lead someone on just for the sake of filling up my social calendar!"

"If your mother were here…"

Now that was a low blow, Joe thought, remembering how hard it had been to get over the loss of his parents.

"Mom would applaud my decision to adopt!" she countered, just as fiercely.

"Your mother, God rest her soul, would be wrong in this instance," Gus snapped.

Hannah shook her head wordlessly and stared at the floor as if praying for strength. She turned back to her father, her composure intact. "When I return, I'm going to have Isabella with me. I'm going to need your support."

It was clear she wasn't going to get it.

The hurt on her face was more than Joe could tolerate. He broke every rule he had about staying out of other people's business. He strode through the aisles and stepped between the warring Callahans. He looked her in the eye. "If we don't want to miss our flight, we better get a move on, Hannah."

Gus looked at Joe with contempt. "You really want to be a friend to her? You'll do everything you can to keep my daughter from *getting on* that plane."

It was easy to see Gus's words cut Hannah like a knife. Joe's temper roiled as the color drained from her face.

Tears sparkled on her lashes, then were promptly blinked back. "Goodbye, Dad," Hannah said hoarsely, stepping forward to give Gus a cursory hug and turning away with a stricken look on her face.

Joe and Hannah walked out to the SUV in silence. Got in.

He felt for her. He knew the pain of wanting a blood relative to love you the way you needed to be loved, only to be turned away. True, his rejection had been a tad more polite. But it had been a rebuff just the same. Joe started the SUV, backed out of the space and headed for the highway.

"Sorry about that." Hannah's hands were shaking.

You shouldn't be, he thought with a wave of feeling that surprised him. Resolutely, he offered what comfort he could. "I've been in some of those orphanages, Hannah." Forty or more cribs sandwiched into a single large room, infants lined up, one after another—sometimes doubling up in a crib—with only one or two attendants to care for them all. "Without people like you, willing to open up their homes and their hearts," he told her gruffly, remembering their sad little faces and haunted eyes, "those kids don't stand a chance."

Hannah exhaled a shaky breath. "My dad…"

"Will come around, once your baby is here," Joe predicted, wishing he could do more to erase the vulnerability on her pretty face.

"You really think so?" She searched his eyes.

Given his own experiences? If Joe were honest, he'd have

to give in to his cynical side and say...no. But that wasn't what Hannah needed to hear.

"Sure," he said. And left it at that.

"THERE MUST BE SOME MISTAKE," a frustrated Hannah told the English-speaking clerk at the registration desk of the five-star Taipei hotel. After thirty-four excruciating hours of travel, she was so tired she could barely function as she held up the index and third finger on her right hand. All she wanted was a hot shower, some clean pajamas...and a comfortable bed. "I asked for two rooms. Not one."

The clerk looked confused. He consulted the computer screen in front of him. "Two adults," he replied in carefully enunciated English, with a slight respectful bow of his head. "Two beds."

"Two adults, two beds, and *two rooms,*" Hannah stipulated as clearly as possible. She turned her hand, palm up, hoping that physical action would accomplish what words had, thus far, not. "So I need *two* electronic key cards."

The clerk looked dumbfounded.

Looking as if he had half-expected in a trip of this magnitude to encounter some kind of glitch, Joe stepped forward and intervened in fluent Mandarin Chinese. Immediately, the clerk began to relax. The two conversed pleasantly for several minutes. Finally, Joe turned to Hannah. "The adoption agency here booked a single room for every 'family' coming in to adopt. You requested separate accommodations for two adults so they gave us a room with two king beds."

That made sense. Sort of. "Can't we get another room?" Hannah asked.

Joe shook his head. "The hotel is fully booked for the rest of the summer. We could try another hotel, but they don't hold out much hope—the nice accommodations are sold out."

She let her head fall back. After a four-hour drive to the El Paso International Airport, a two-hour preflight wait, twenty-six hours in the air to Taipei, and another three hours getting through customs and to the hotel, she was dead on her feet. Joe had napped off and on, but she had barely slept on the plane. She was too nervous and excited about her future.

"One room is fine," Joe said.

The thought of sharing space lent an intimacy to the trip she had not expected. "But…" Hannah protested.

Exhaustion tautened the lines of his face. "We'll survive, Hannah. Besides, everyone adopting through the agency you're using is on the fifth floor. You're going to need to be there when they bring the babies up tomorrow afternoon."

Hannah knew that was true. She looked at Joe. This was not what he had signed on for, either. "I'm really sorry."

He picked up both suitcases and strode across the spectacular marble lobby to the elevators. "All I want is a shower and a place to lay my head. Anything else, at this point, is extraneous."

To Hannah's relief, the accommodations were beautiful and luxurious. The room was spacious with a spectacular wall of glass windows overlooking the city. The beds were huge and made up with beautiful linens, goose down comforters and feather pillows. The suite also had a plasma TV, writing desk and chair and a high-speed Internet connection. The adjoining bathroom had twin sinks, marble shower and soaking tub.

Joe, it would appear, could have cared less about the accommodations. He headed for the complimentary fruit basket on the desk. He grabbed an apple with one hand, set his laptop on the desk with the other. "I've got to check my e-mail so if you want the bath, it's all yours."

She wanted a shower more than she could say. She dragged her suitcase into the bathroom, made good use of the free scented soaps and shampoo, then stood under the spray, letting the soothing warmth seep into her bones.

Tired enough to fall asleep standing up, she got out, wrapped her wet hair in a towel and donned one of the thick white hotel robes. Staying up only long enough to brush her teeth and run a comb through her wet hair, she emerged and stumbled wearily into the closest bed. Her head hit the pillow and she closed her eyes.

"THEY'RE NOT THAT LATE, HANNAH," Joe chided at two the following afternoon, not sure when a night and half a day had passed with such excruciating slowness. Mainly because ever since they'd been closeted together, he'd had a hard time taking his eyes off his suite mate.

Oblivious to the errant nature of his thoughts, Hannah consulted her watch and continued to pace. "The van from the orphanage was supposed to be here nearly half an hour ago."

And during that time she had paced back and forth in front of the windows so many times Joe had her spectacular legs—and the inherent sexiness of her feminine stride—memorized. He shifted his glance upward, past her perfectly shaped torso to the silky brown hair brushing her slender shoulders. Her arms were incredibly toned, too. "Maybe they got stuck in traffic."

"Then why haven't they called to let us know?" she asked in a distressed voice.

He shrugged and looked directly into her long-lashed brown eyes. "Could be any number of reasons," he said, wishing she had chosen to wear anything but that alluring white dress. "I'm certain everything is fine," he repeated, reminding himself this situation had no room for desire on either of their parts.

"You're right." Hannah bit into her lower lip. Her delicate cheeks flushed with emotion. "I'm overreacting." Exasperated, she propped her hands on her hips. "Not that this is your problem, in any case."

It sure wasn't supposed to be, Joe reflected. And it wouldn't be now if a last-minute family emergency hadn't kept Hannah's friend from Chicago, who had already adopted a little girl from Taiwan, from making the trip. But her friend had been forced to cancel, and the international adoption agency Hannah was using insisted all of the infants being adopted be escorted back to their new countries by two responsible adults. Which, Joe admitted, was not a bad idea given the sheer distance most of the international adoptees and their new parents were traveling.

Hannah's only family was Gus. Even if Gus had wanted to go, his health issues would have prevented such a long journey.

So she had asked Joe if he would consider going with her. Hannah had assured him he would not have to do anything regarding her adoption of the infant. While she was getting acquainted with her child and taking care of all the adoption and immigration legalities, he could stay in the hotel room and work on the magazine articles tied to his latest book project as well as indulge in as much of the culture as he wanted.

That had all sounded good to him. He had been in Summit, Texas, too long and he loved this part of Asia.

Unfortunately, the reservation mix-up had hampered his ability to concentrate and left him acutely aware of many things. The rosewood and patchouli fragrance of Hannah's soap and shampoo. The fact she carried a stick of lip balm and applied it, every hour or so. The knowledge that the treatment worked—her full lips were a healthy pink and seductively soft. Too soft, Joe chided himself sternly, for him to be thinking about when they were cooped up this way.

The phone rang. Hannah jumped and rushed to pick it up. She listened intently, then smiled in relief. She thanked the caller, hung up and turned to him. "There was a problem with the conference room where we were all supposed to meet, so—" She paused as a knock sounded on the hotel room door. "Oh my God. Joe! She's here!"

Chapter Two

Her heart in her throat, Hannah rushed toward the door and flung it open. On the other side of the portal, a Taiwanese nanny stood, with Hannah's baby in her arms. For a second, Hannah was so overwhelmed with emotion, she could barely breathe. Her daughter was here—at long last.

And the baby was *so* much smaller than Hannah had expected. Only about fourteen pounds, at ten months of age. She was also absolutely, incredibly beautiful. Dark almond-shaped eyes were framed by long thick lashes and nestled beneath thin expressive brows. Her nose was cute and pert, her bow-shaped lips unexpectedly solemn. Her round little face was fuller than it had been in the photo that had been sent months ago, her bone structure more delicately feminine, and her legs and arms were almost alarmingly limp and thin. Her golden skin was flushed pink and it was easy to see why—her child was way too warmly dressed for a summer day. But this, too, Hannah had learned was typical. The Taiwanese feared children becoming chilled and catching cold. Hence, infants here were always quite warmly dressed, no matter what the season.

"This is Zhu Ming," the nanny said, as the same scene was repeated at doors up and down the hotel corridor.

"Hello, Isabella Zhu Ming," Hannah whispered tenderly, holding out her arms. The nanny gently made the transfer. Inundated with the love she'd felt for months, Hannah smoothed a tuft of wispy black hair from her little girl's cheek and held her close.

In response, wariness gleamed in her daughter's dark eyes, resistance tautened her body. Her baby wasn't struggling to get away, but she wasn't melting into her embrace, either, Hannah noted in disappointment. Rather, she regarded her with a world-weary resignation that went far beyond her age.

It's going to take time for her to adjust and to trust that you won't leave her, too, Hannah had been warned.

Intellectually, she'd braced herself for just this situation, many times over. Still, she felt momentarily shaken by her child's stoic resistance.

The nanny handed over a diaper bag containing formula, rice cereal and half a dozen diapers. "We return at nine in morning, escort you to local court, finalize adoption." The nanny touched Isabella's cheek. "*Zaijian,* Zhu Ming."

Isabella's lower lip trembled at the nanny's soft goodbye. She looked even more frightened and uncertain as the woman walked away and the door shut gently behind her.

Hannah caught a glimpse of Joe's expression—he seemed as transfixed and in awe as she—then turned her full attention back to the child of her dreams.

"It's all right, sweetheart," she soothed, walking slowly toward the windows overlooking the city. She'd hoped the view would soothe the little girl. Instead, the view of the tall, elegant buildings made Isabella Zhu Ming all the more anxious. Tears eked out of the corners of her infant's eyes. She wasn't making a sound, but she was clearly very distressed.

And no wonder, she thought, her heart going out to her

sweet little baby girl. Isabella Zhu Ming probably hadn't been out of the orphanage since she was abandoned in a market-place, the previous autumn. To be dressed in clothes that were way too warm, driven several hours on a bus and then to be promptly handed over to a stranger who didn't even speak her own language had to be very frightening indeed.

Resolved to make this transition as easy as possible, Hannah continued walking her baby about the hotel room, gently rubbing her back and speaking softly. "We've got all the time in the world, my sweet baby girl. Your momma's here, and I promise from here on out I'll do everything in my power to protect you so you never feel abandoned ever again."

JOE'D THOUGHT EVERY OUNCE of overwrought sentimentality had been wrung out of him in the year after his parents' death. He didn't cry, period. So it was a shock to feel his throat tight-ening as he watched Hannah interact with her baby for the very first time.

There was something so tender in the way she held the child.

Something equally moving in the way the child was re-sponding to her.

Which went to show how much a mother's love could mean.

And Hannah did love this child she had barely met. That was apparent. The two were already bonding, albeit slowly and cautiously on Isabella Zhu Ming's part.

Noting the way the baby had started chewing and sucking on her tiny fist, Hannah retrieved the bag of essential items the nanny had left. With her free hand, Hannah perused what was inside the canvas knapsack. Still cuddling the baby close to her breasts, she paused to read a typewritten set of instructions.

Wordlessly, Hannah hazarded a glance at Joe, who was

trying without much success to get back to work, then frowned as she walked back over to the bed to put the baby down.

As soon as the baby hit the feather comforter, she began to cry.

"Oh, dear." Hannah immediately picked the infant back up again.

Isabella stopped crying and held on to her for dear life.

Hannah looked at Joe. "I know I promised I wouldn't ask..."

Uh-oh.

"...but according to the schedule, Isabella is supposed to have a bottle of soy formula at 4 p.m. I need to get the bottle ready and check her diaper and see if it's wet, and since this is all so new to her..."

Hannah looked so tortured about having to make the request, he let her off the hook with a casual offer of assistance. "You want me to hold her?" he said as if it were no big deal, when it felt like it was going to be a very big deal.

Hannah nodded, looking emotional again. "Would you, please? Just for a moment?" she asked in a low, quavering tone.

He held out his arms.

Isabella went into them with a suspicious look. When Hannah eased away, Isabella continued to glare at him. Surprised at the tenderness welling up inside of him, Joe offered his little finger. Still scowling, the baby stared at it for a long minute, then thrust out her lower lip petulantly and latched on to it with one tiny fist.

Joe looked into eyes that held far too much cynicism for someone so young. He tried—and failed—to coax even a hint of a smile from her. "I don't think she likes me as much as she likes you," he teased.

Hannah lifted her brows accepting the lighthearted comment with the sentiment with which it had been made. Turning back to her task, she prepared the bottle with powdered soy formula and boiled water from the thermos that was standard in all Taiwanese hotel rooms. "She probably just hasn't been around many men. I think all the workers in the orphanages are women."

"I hadn't thought of that." Joe regretted his pass on the razor that morning. He lifted Isabella's tiny hand to his stubble and saw her frown as if perplexed. "You probably think I should have shaved prior to our introduction, huh?"

Isabella stared at Joe, wide-eyed.

At least for the moment, Joe thought, she was distracted from her hunger...

Hannah fastened the nipple onto the mouth of the plastic baby bottle and twisted tight. As she approached them, she grinned and tilted her head a little to one side to survey him better. "You do look a little like a pirate," she said thoughtfully.

Aware the dramatic repartee was working to entertain the solemn child, Joe pretended to be incensed. "You hear that, Isabella Zhu Ming? I think I've just been insulted!"

Isabella turned to Hannah, as if waiting to see her reaction to Joe's assertion.

Hannah did not disappoint. She made a face that was just as comical—and just as interesting to little Isabella.

"No, you weren't!" Hannah scoffed, peering at Joe and then Isabella. "Pirates are sexy!"

"Are we talking about me now—or the actors in the *Pirates of the Caribbean* movies?" He glided closer.

Hannah shook the bottle vigorously, blushing all the while. "Orlando Bloom, of course. I've always had a bit of a crush on him and he made an incredible swashbuckler."

Good to know Hannah hadn't been hitting on him just now, Joe thought wryly. No sense in setting either of them up for disappointment. Not that he had ever expected anything to come of his association with Hannah, anyway. She was putting down roots in her hometown. He had nowhere to go back to and didn't really want a home base. Traveling was easier. Roaming around the way he did, there was no expectation of belonging. All that was required was that he fit in temporarily, and then move on, without looking back. He was an ace at that.

Hannah tested the formula on her wrist. "Whoa. They told us to use the boiled water in the hotel thermoses for making formula, but this is going to have to cool off for a minute."

Too late, Isabella had seen the bottle. Making no bones about how hungry she was, she reached out her hands and when it didn't come right away, began to cry.

"Hang on, little one, it's coming," Hannah soothed, wincing at the sound of the baby's high-pitched, heartbreaking sobs. She rushed to put the bottle under cool running water. After a minute or so beneath the tap, the formula had cooled enough for her to give Isabella the bottle. Once Joe handed the baby back to her, Isabella took the bottle between her little hands and sucked greedily.

In two minutes flat, the bottle was empty.

Isabella looked back at Hannah, clearly wanting more. Hannah seemed nonplussed. "Should we fix her another bottle?"

She was asking him? What did he know about babies, except how to hold one in an emergency? "Sounds fine to me," he said, returning the decision to her.

HANNAH DIDN'T KNOW WHAT HAD gotten into her. She had been preparing for this day for months now, yet she was suddenly all flustered. Worse, she knew why. From the moment they'd first met, she'd always been a little too aware of Joe.

And it was more than just his appearance—which was very appealing in itself. But, ultimately it was the sophistication that came from seeing so much of the world. The way he knew when to come a little closer, and when to back off. It was the kindness in his eyes, the gentleness in his touch, and the way Isabella looked up at him, completely spellbound after just a few minutes in his strong arms.

He would have been the perfect father to her baby.

If only he'd been interested in having a family…which he wasn't.

She needed to remember that. And she needed to stop *leaning* on him, asking him to help her get Isabella settled in.

"Want me to hold her while you fix another bottle?" Joe asked.

It was now or never. She had told everyone she could do this as a single mother. It was time to prove it. Hannah drew a bolstering breath. "Actually, I think we're fine. So if you want to do anything else…see the sights, go out to dinner… it'd be fine. *We'll* be fine."

For a second, Joe's expression didn't change. Then, ever so subtly, a veil came over his emotions. Once again, he became the Joe who had picked her up two days ago. The Joe who had taken her to the airport and sat in a different section of the airplane. The Joe who was there to escort her to and from Taiwan and nothing more.

"Good idea." He flashed her a handsome grin that filled her senses. "You two probably want time to settle in."

Oblivious to her disappointment, he pocketed his electronic room key and gave her a wink. "Don't wait up."

IN THE HOURS THAT FOLLOWED, Hannah had plenty of time to regret her decision to send Joe off into the nightlife of Taipei.

The first moment came when she realized she only had enough powder for one more bottle, and Isabella didn't like the taste of the American-made soy formula she had brought with her. Fortunately, one of the other adoptive families on the floor had anticipated this and made a run to the closest grocery for more. They shared their extra with Hannah.

The next problem was not so easily solved.

She was still contemplating what to do about it when Joe returned four hours later. He walked in, saw her sitting in a chair, Isabella cradled in her arms.

He lifted one blond brow. "Still awake?"

Fatigue fighting with the contentment deep inside her, Hannah nodded. "Oh, yeah."

Joe set his room key, wallet and BlackBerry on top of the bureau. He toed off his loafers, then came over to sit on the side of the bed, opposite her. He braced his elbows on his thighs. Leaning closer, his expression softened as his gaze moved over the fully alert baby snuggled contentedly in her arms. "That's not a good thing?"

Hannah didn't have a lot of experience with infants. But… "In the orphanage she would have been asleep two hours ago, or so the schedule says."

Joe shifted his gaze from Isabella Zhu Ming to Hannah. "Then what happened?"

Hannah flushed at his scrutiny. "I'm not sure."

He returned his attention to the baby. "What do you know?"

Hannah made a face that mirrored her inner frustration at having apparently failed as a mother so soon. A good mother, she felt, would have been able to take charge immediately, rather than be at the mercy of emotions in her baby she couldn't quite soothe. She inclined her head at Isabella. "I can't get her to sleep and I can't put her down."

Joe took a moment to consider that. "If you can't put her down, how do you change her diaper?" he asked eventually.

Despite her efforts to play it cool, ruefulness crept into her tone. "With great difficulty."

Joe eyed the telltale stains on her white dress. "I see what you mean," he remarked dryly, knowing as well as Hannah she couldn't sit there forever. "So what's the plan?" he asked.

"I was going to try and bathe her in the hopes that the warm water would relax her."

Joe seemed to concur that it was a good plan. "But…?"

Hannah swallowed, aware she was beginning to feel over-whelmed by all she didn't know and had yet to experience. "Isabella's never had an actual bath in a tub or sink. The care-takers wipe them down with washcloths in the orphanage."

Compassion lit his eyes. "You think she's going to freak?"

Unfortunately, yes. "It had occurred to me."

He squinted. "What happened to her hair?"

Hannah looked down at the top of Isabella's head. "I rubbed baby oil into her scalp, to soften the cradle cap."

Joe moved to stand beside Hannah. "It looks soft, all right."

As well as greasy. "Obviously, I need to shampoo that out."

Looking more man of action than uninvolved bystander, Joe braced his hands on his waist. "Hard to do if you can't put her down," he noted.

Hannah didn't want Isabella screaming in terror before she even got her in the water. Nor could she do everything with one hand, while still holding Isabella with the other. "Exactly."

Joe sized up the situation. "Want me to help?"

He didn't know how much. Yet, her conscience prevailed. "I promised you that you wouldn't have to do this stuff," Hannah reminded him guiltily.

Joe's lips tightened with determination. "Let me put it to you this way. If she doesn't sleep, you don't sleep. And if neither of you sleep, I won't sleep...and I like to sleep. So, what do you say we get this show on the road? Where do you want to do this?" he asked.

Hannah sized up the accommodations. The bathtub was way too big and deep for a baby who couldn't even sit up yet. "How about the sink?"

"Good choice." Joe cleared the toiletries from the marble counter between the two sinks. "She can look at herself in the mirror."

Hannah turned the infant so that Isabella could see her reflection. The smile she had hoped to see did not come, but Isabella kept her gaze on the mirror. "If you could hold her, I can get everything ready."

Joe held out his hands. Their hands and arms touched as they shifted the baby from her embrace to his. Isabella's brows knit together, but she did not make a sound.

Hannah spread a thick hotel towel on the counter, and draped the baby bath towel on top of that. She brought in a bottle of lavender-scented baby wash and shampoo, a small thin baby washcloth, a clean diaper, undershirt and sleeper. Joe swayed the baby back and forth in his arms until the shallow oval basin was filled with warm water.

Hannah turned to him, aware she was nervous again. Maybe because it had never been more important to her to do something right. "I'll ease her clothes off while you hold her."

"Sounds good."

Gently, she eased the pants and sweater Isabella had been wearing from her body. The diaper, after that. It was the first time Hannah had seen her baby without any clothing. She was shocked by how thin Isabella's arms were, but relieved to see her torso was nice and sturdy, her ribs barely discernible beneath her delicate golden skin.

Hannah checked Joe to see if he was ready. He looked back at her as if to say, *Here goes.*

Murmuring soft words of comfort, Hannah eased Isabella Zhu Ming into the warm water. Isabella stiffened, a look of terror on her face, and began to struggle hysterically to get out. Joe produced the yellow rubber ducky. Isabella batted it away, still kicking.

He began speaking in Mandarin Chinese.

Isabella grew very still.

He did a little puppet show. "*Huaji* rubber ducky. Rubber ducky *xihuan,* Isabella Zhu Ming…"

He made quacking sounds that had Hannah smiling, Isabella solemn but intent. He had the duck "swim" circles around Isabella and washed the rubber ducky's beak with the same baby wash Hannah was using on Isabella. By the time Hannah had put the shampoo in Isabella's hair and tenderly massaged it in, Isabella was less concerned with the newness of her bath, reaching tentatively for the duck. She had it clutched in her hand by the time Hannah rinsed the soap out with a cup of water. Joe and Hannah locked eyes. They shared the triumph of her first bath, which, thanks to his help, had been relatively stress-free.

Isabella was still holding on to the toy when Hannah drew her out and wrapped her in a hooded towel. Soundlessly, Isabella examined every aspect of the duck while Hannah dressed her in a soft pink cotton sleeper. Hannah picked her up and breathed in the soft, clean baby scent of her. Tenderness, unlike anything she had ever felt, filled her heart. And she could have sworn, Joe felt it, too…

JOE HAD HEARD IT COULD TAKE days, weeks…even months for an adoptive mother to bond with an older infant.

Obviously, he noted as Hannah cuddled Isabella Zhu Ming Callahan close to her heart, this was not the case here. There was an unspoken connection between the two that transcended the barrier of so much that was unfamiliar. They communicated with touch and look. The message both were sending out was that they belonged together.

"You look so…wistful," Hannah remarked, reluctantly handing Isabella back to Joe so she could make another bottle of formula.

"Do I?" He cradled Isabella in his arms and found the experience of holding the sweet and solemn little girl every bit as fulfilling as Hannah evidently had. Was this how it felt to be a parent? Was he giving up something incredible in refusing even to consider the possibility of fathering a child? Or was he being smart, given the kind of life he led, in abandoning the idea of a family of his own?

Finished making the bottle, Hannah retrieved Isabella and sat down in one of the upholstered chairs in front of the windows.

"You do." She offered the bottle to Isabella. Once again, the baby turned her head away from Hannah to drink it. She stared at Joe instead.

Restless, Joe got up and took one of the chocolates the hotel staff had left on his pillow at turndown. "I was just thinking about how much of the world I have left to see and write about," he fibbed, sure the unexpected sentiment he felt would disappear the moment they got back to the States and parted company once again.

Hannah shifted so the baby would be situated more

comfortably in her arms. "How many books have you done so far?"

Joe picked up the camera she had brought with her and took a couple of photos he knew she would appreciate later. "Ten."

Hannah smiled as the baby snuggled closer and shut her eyes. "How many do you intend to do?"

He shrugged, intent on capturing that moment of sweet mother-daughter bonding. He knelt and used the zoom function on the lens. "Fifty, if I'm lucky, plus updated versions of all the books I have in print."

Hannah considered him thoughtfully. "Which means you go back to the countries you've already detailed?"

Wishing the two of them were like-minded enough to date, Joe nodded. "Right. I add new places, take out others that have either declined or closed their doors." Desire welled inside him. He shunted it aside deliberately.

Compassion lit Hannah's dark-brown eyes. "It must be exciting."

And lonely, he thought. Especially on nights like this, when he was in an incredible city and had no one special to share it with. He turned the attention back to her once again. "You traveled a lot in your previous job, didn't you?"

Hannah shifted the baby to her shoulder. "Every week I went somewhere to meet with a customer and help them revise or completely retool the marketing plan for their business."

"Did you like it?"

Hannah patted Isabella gently on the back. "I liked the challenge of figuring out how to make something better." She scowled, admitting, "I hated living out of a suitcase in so-so hotel rooms, always getting in late—or having to leave very early—driving rental cars in unfamiliar cities...."

Joe grinned. "I'm getting the sense you didn't enjoy the traveling part," he teased.

"You sense right. Although," she added pensively, "maybe it would have been different if five-star accommodations and chauffeured limos had been part of my expense account." She sneaked a peek at the infant curled up on her shoulder. "I think she's finally asleep."

"Want to try and put her down?"

Hannah nodded.

Joe took the empty baby bottle from her hand, being careful not to touch her in the process. She rose slowly, Isabella still in her arms, glided ever so carefully over to the port-a-crib in the corner, and gingerly eased Isabella down on her back.

To their mutual relief, Isabella slept on.

The picture of maternal tenderness, Hannah took the pink cotton baby quilt with the satin trim and tucked it around her new daughter. Next to her child, she secured the rubber ducky and an infant-size teddy bear, so both would be within reach when Isabella did wake up.

Hannah stepped back, still looking down at her daughter. Joe was so busy admiring her skill as a mother, he didn't get out of her way fast enough. Their bodies brushed. She tilted her face up to his. Their glances met, and it was all Joe could do to keep from taking her into his arms, lowering his mouth to hers. The rational side of him knew, however, that kissing her now would be out of line. The last thing he wanted to do was take advantage of her, or the situation.

Pushing his own desire aside once again, Joe cleared his throat, stepped back. He wished the situation were different, he were different. Because if he were a stay-in-one-place kind of guy he wouldn't hesitate to make a move on Hannah, to see if this simmering attraction he'd been feeling led anywhere. But he wasn't in the market for a wife and kid. And she wasn't the kind of woman looking to have a fleeting affair. It was best, then, that they stayed friends. And only friends. "Guess we better hit the sack while we can," he stated affably.

Hannah's dreamy expression faded. In complete control of her emotions once again, she nodded. "No telling how long she'll sleep."

Joe walked over to the bureau where he had stowed his things. On top was his BlackBerry. Before he attached it to the charger, he checked the screen, saw the text message. He exhaled, resigned, and turned back to her. "I have to make a call. I'll go downstairs."

"You can do that here," she offered.

Joe dreaded the upcoming conversation. This was not a part of his life he wished to share, even inadvertently. "I don't want to chance waking Isabella up." He pocketed his hotel room key card and warned without inflection, "I may be a while. So don't feel you have to wait up."

Chapter Three

Hannah got ready for bed and climbed beneath the covers. She should have been exhausted since it had been such an eventful day. What kept her awake was the look on Joe's face when he checked his BlackBerry…the way he'd had to leave the room to make a phone call.

She understood he might want his privacy.

Furthermore, she knew she had no right to be curious about what was going on in his life tonight.

And yet…she was.

Did he have a woman in his life?

He hadn't mentioned one.

No one had seen him with a female friend in the four months he had been renting a cabin outside of Summit. But that didn't mean he wasn't romantically involved.

She had just assumed, by the quick way he had accepted her invitation to accompany her to Taiwan, that he was single and as unencumbered emotionally as she was.

Although she did not know why this should suddenly matter to her. The two of them were not hooking up. He was moving on shortly after they returned to Texas.

And yet the way he had stopped dead in his tracks when

he had read the message, not to mention the byplay of emotion across his face, made her sure he was dealing with something very personal.

As she drifted off to sleep, Hannah was still wondering what could have caused him to react like that.

The next thing she knew, she was waking to the hysterical shriek of the baby in the crib beside her bed. She bolted upright, as Isabella screamed in terror. Hannah flung back the covers. In the opposite bed, Joe did the same. Hannah picked up Isabella, soothing her with words and touch. To no avail. Isabella looked at Hannah as if she had never seen her before in her life. Tears streaming from her dark eyes, she screamed and kicked and flailed. Joe turned on a light.

He came toward them, rubbing the sleep from his eyes. "What is it?"

"I don't know." Hannah walked Isabella back and forth. She gently rubbed her daughter's back, soothing her all the while. "I think it might be a night terror." She had read about the sleep disturbance in infants. "She looks like she's awake…"

"But she's really still in the midst of a nightmare." Joe spoke to be heard above the crying.

Hannah nodded.

He began speaking Mandarin Chinese. Hannah had no idea what he was saying, but the sound of his low, masculine voice soothed Isabella—and Hannah—in a way her English words could not.

As Hannah continued to sway the baby back and forth, Joe kept murmuring to her child. Slowly, the wailing diminished, and the tears stopped flowing. Before long, Isabella's eyes slowly shut again.

Her own body relaxing in relief, Hannah held her baby close, rocking her gently back and forth, letting the rise and fall of her own chest synch with Isabella's. Until finally, her little girl was limp in her arms once again. Hannah carefully eased Isabella back into the port-a-crib and covered her with a blanket.

Trembling with delayed reaction to the tumultuous event, Hannah sat down on the side of the bed.

Her heart still racing, she watched over her baby for signs of further distress. There were none.

Concerned, Joe brought her a bottle of water.

Hannah drank deeply. He touched her shoulder briefly, his palm as warm and comforting against her bare skin as his verbal reassurances had been to her infant daughter.

"Try and get some sleep," he whispered.

Feeling like she could drown in the empathy in his eyes, knowing it would be all too easy to depend on his inherent kindness, she nodded. Seconds later, they turned off the light.

As Hannah lay back against the pillows, her breath shallow in her chest, she wondered what had frightened the baby so. Was Isabella remembering the night she had been abandoned in a city park by the family who could not care for her? Nights and days spent in an orphanage where again it seemed like she was all alone? Or was she afraid of the changes and unfamiliar faces?

All Hannah knew for sure was that she would do anything to protect her baby. Isabella needed to know she had family now. A family who would always love her and care for her, a family she could count on.

Isabella would never be forsaken again, Hannah vowed fiercely. She would see to that.

"WHAT DO YOU MEAN THERE'S going to be a delay?" Hannah asked the international adoption agency representative who had come to their suite.

Joe turned to the bearer of bad news.

The Hong Kong–born woman in charge of all legal matters was deeply apologetic. "We have just received word that our English interpreter has fallen ill. Our appointment with the local court is in one hour. We cannot get a suitable replacement that quickly. So all the English-speaking families in the group will have to reschedule for next week. The French and Italian families will proceed as scheduled."

Joe watched the color drain from Hannah's cheeks. He could imagine what she was thinking. International adoptions were orchestrated very carefully. A single glitch could cause the process to be set back for weeks or months. A lengthy delay would not only cost her thousands of additional dollars she might not have to spend, it could also prompt the Taiwanese authorities to send Isabella Zhu Ming back to the orphanage, until all was in order again.

Any obstacle to Isabella legally becoming Hannah's child was unbearable. "Can't you act as interpreter?" she asked the woman emotionally.

The representative shook her head. "While my English is fine, my Mandarin is rudimentary. The magistrate will be asking questions, and your answers to him must be correctly translated."

Once again, Joe found himself getting involved despite his better judgment. "I speak the language fluently." Before he knew it, he was on his way to the local court with the rest of the group. And Hannah Callahan was looking at him with more gratitude than ever before....

Once the adoptive families arrived, they were ushered into a waiting room and then called in to the judge's chambers, one by one.

Joe served as interpreter for two other families before it

was Hannah's turn to appear with Isabella. As in other cases before the magistrate, vital statistics for both were verified. Then came the questions that were even more important.

"Are you adopting this baby girl as a single parent?"

"I am," Hannah answered.

Her reply was translated. Then the next question came and was similarly transposed so she could understand. "Do you plan to someday marry?" Joe inquired for the court.

Hannah hesitated, her eyes locking with his momentarily, before she turned back to the bench. And in the silence that fell Joe found he was—surprisingly—almost as interested to hear her reply as the judge.

"I will only marry if the man loves Isabella as much as I do and will promise to be there for her always," Hannah stated plainly.

Her answer was relayed. The judge nodded, his gaze approving—but stern. Another question in Mandarin.

Again, Joe translated. "Who will care for this child?"

Hannah's voice rang with the certainty of a promise made and kept. "I will."

"Will you be with the child during the day or will you be at work?" was the judge's next inquiry.

"I will take the baby with me to the store where I work. I can do this," she explained, "because my family owns the store."

Gus might have something to say about that, Joe thought. Then again, given the look of determination on Hannah's face, maybe Gus would not have a say, at all....

"Do you promise to love this child always?"

As soon as she understood the question, Hannah's heart was in her voice, and her eyes shone with tears. "Yes. I will always love her."

"Do you promise to never abandon her?" Joe asked for the

judge, looking deep into Hannah's eyes. Yet already knowing the answer as surely as he was beginning to know her.

"I promise that with all my heart," she said thickly. And this time a single tear—of pure and unadulterated happiness—did fall.

To HANNAH'S DELIGHT, ISABELLA Zhu Ming Callahan's adoption was approved and her HHR—household registry—was changed to reflect this. The adoption then became legal and final. And it was off to a clinic with the rest of the babies to have a rudimentary physical examination that consisted of a palpitation of her abdomen, a listen to her heart and lungs, a measurement of her head, and movement of her arms and legs.

That quickly, she was pronounced healthy, a rubber stamp affixed to the required medical exam papers. After the groups split up to keep their preset appointments with the various consulates, the three of them headed to the American Institute in Taiwan. In the consular section on the third floor, another interview commenced—this one all in English—and an immigrant visa was issued for Isabella Zhu Ming Callahan.

Hannah didn't know whose smile was broader—hers or Joe's—as they left the AIT. It had been six hours since they had left the hotel, and although Isabella had enjoyed several bottles of formula, neither she nor Joe had eaten. The hotel was a half-hour cab ride away. The dinner hour was upon them. Aware what a trooper he'd been, and how little she'd done to see to his comfort on this trip, she offered a tentative smile. "We should celebrate," she said.

Joe grinned back, looking more content and at ease than she had ever seen him. "We should," he agreed.

The question was where, she thought, acutely aware that this was suddenly feeling more like an impromptu date than a mission to be accomplished. "Any ideas?" she asked, trying not to notice how strong and handsome Joe looked standing there beside her.

Joe slid his hands in his trouser pockets. "We could have dinner at a place I know." He maintained the casual attitude he'd exuded all day. "It's not too fancy but the food is amazing."

Wishing she had time to freshen up, Hannah used her free hand to push the hair from her face. "Sounds great."

There was no chance to converse en route because Joe was busy giving the driver directions in Mandarin Chinese. Upon arrival, Hannah took Isabella to the ladies' room to change her damp diaper. When she returned, Joe was on his cell. He looked…stressed.

"I think you should calm down." He shot her an apologetic look for the interruption and kept right on giving counsel. "Girls that age break up with their boyfriends all the time. If Valerie thinks it was time for Elliott to hit the road, then I'm sure it was. Yeah, I will. But I don't think she's going to call me. Bye, Aunt Camille."

His expression taut with displeasure, he ended the connection and addressed her. "Sorry about that. I'd had about ten messages from them today. I really needed to call my aunt and uncle back."

Although very open about many aspects of his life, Joe had said very little about his family. She was glad he'd brought it up. "You're close to them?"

For a second, Joe hesitated. His expression became even more circumspect. "They became my guardians when my mom and dad were killed in a train derailment while on vacation in Spain."

Hannah knew how hard it had been, losing her mom just two years ago. It had to have been much tougher for him to lose both parents at once. "How old were you?" she asked sympathetically.

"Nine." He looked over at Isabella, and she leaned toward him, indicating she wanted to go to him for a while. "I lived with my aunt and uncle and their three kids for about a year, and then I went to a boarding school after that." He held out his arms to the baby.

"Was going away to school a tradition in your family?" she asked, handing Isabella to him.

He propped Isabella against his shoulder, so she could look out at the other patrons in the small homey restaurant. She rested her cheek against his shirt, wreathed one arm about his neck and clutched his sleeve with her other hand.

"I'm the only one who went." Joe surveyed Hannah while he cuddled Isabella close, the tenderness of the gesture bringing a lump to Hannah's throat. "But it was a good experience," he continued matter-of-factly. "It made me independent at an early age."

Independent, or unable to settle down? Hannah wondered. Trying not to think how sad that was, she mixed formula in the baby bottle, capped it with the nipple and shook it vigorously.

Joe leaned back, allowing the waitress to put the menus in front of them. "Anyway, yesterday the family discovered that Valerie dropped out of summer classes and moved out of her college dorm without discussing it with them first."

"Why would she do that?" Ready to feed the baby, Hannah held out her arms.

Joe slid Isabella into her embrace. "Apparently, she and her boyfriend broke up. She decided she could no longer be on the same campus as he was—they were both in summer school at a private liberal arts college just outside Austin. She contacted the registrar, told them she was quitting the university and took off."

She situated Isabella with the bottle. Again the baby faced away from her, as was her preference while she fed. "And no one told her parents?"

The waitress appeared with two cups of green tea. "Valerie told her student advisor she was going to do that."

"But she didn't." Hannah pointed to what she wanted on the menu.

Joe placed his order, then continued catching her up. "Valerie told them about the breakup—she didn't tell them about the dropping-out-of-school part. So when my aunt and uncle flew down from their summer place in Aspen yesterday to check on Valerie and found out what happened, they were livid. They found her staying with one of her girlfriends in San Antonio and demanded she meet with them immediately. She said no and took off again to parts unknown."

Joe exhaled in frustration. "Ten minutes after the conversation with my aunt—who can be a little, uh, shall we say controlling—Valerie withdrew enough cash from her ATM to last her a while. Anyway, that's why they were so desperate to talk to me last night and why I went down to the lobby to return their call. They thought she might try to stay with me, since I've been living in Texas temporarily."

Isabella finished her bottle. Hannah sat her up on her lap, facing Joe. "Only you're not in Texas right now."

"But Valerie doesn't know that, since I didn't tell the family I would be over here with you." He paused, explaining, "When they need me, they contact me by e-mail...or cell. Other than that, we don't communicate a lot."

Isabella burped softly, a bubble of milk covered her lower lip. Joe leaned over and dabbed it with a cloth napkin.

Hannah smiled at the display of tenderness. He was a natural, when it came to kids. "Are you and Valerie close?" she asked curiously.

Again, that self-protective expression. "Let's just say we have similar standings in the family," Joe remarked quietly.

Similar standings? What did that mean? And why did she see a flash of sorrow in his eyes just now?

"Anyway, I'm sure she's fine." Joe's emotions were veiled again. "My cousin will turn up—but not until she is ready."

Joe spent the rest of the meal regaling her with tales of his exploits in China and Taiwan. Just hearing about his experiences thrilled Hannah, and it was with great reluctance that they returned to their suite.

Hannah stood slightly to the side as Joe unlocked the door with the electronic key card. "Thank you for a wonderful dinner."

He held the door for her, his tall body radiating warmth and strength. "Thanks for the company." He stepped back to let her pass, then followed her inside. He shut the door behind them, the action cloaking them in the intimacy of shared space.

He smiled. "I can't remember when I've had two such charming dinner companions." Coming near once more, Joe tucked his index finger into Isabella's fist. Isabella looked up at him with the solemn expression Hannah was beginning to love so much.

Regretting the fact that their time together was about to end, Hannah asked him wistfully, "Do you think she'll ever smile?"

Joe nodded, as certain as Hannah was unsure. "She will when she's sure she's here to stay. That this isn't all some wonderful dream she's having."

His affection for her child kindled feelings in Hannah— for him. She kicked off her shoes and sank down onto the edge of the bed, with Isabella still in her arms. "She is wonderful, isn't she?"

Joe sat down next to Hannah and smoothed a hand through Isabella's soft hair. "And then some."

For a moment they reveled in the wonder of the child they had both come to know.

They studied one another. Hannah couldn't be sure, but she thought—hoped—Joe was fighting a desire to take her in his arms and kiss her. The same way she was fighting not to kiss him.

Working hard to keep her feelings in check, she turned her glance to the suitcases that still had to be packed. "And tomorrow we go back to Texas." To real life. Away from the fantasy and wonder of this magical time in Taiwan...

Joe caught her hand in his. "I thought you'd be happier about that."

She looked down at their entwined palms. It was a friendly gesture. Nothing more. Yet his touch felt so good...so right. "I'm worried about my dad," she admitted.

He squeezed her hand reassuringly before letting go. "Gus is going to love Isabella when he sees her."

Hannah gave Joe a skeptical look.

"How could he not?" he asked.

How, indeed? Hannah wondered.

"YOU SURE YOU WANT ME TO GO IN with you?" Joe guided his Land Rover into a space in front of Callahan Mercantile & Feed.

Gus's truck was still out front, Hannah noted. Which was no surprise. Her dad often went in early, getting there at least an hour before the 7:00 a.m. opening, and staying at least an hour after it closed for the day. Sundays were a little lighter,

but he was still there at least eight hours. The schedule, plus
his refusal to ever take a vacation—never mind retire—had
contributed to his heart attack. Hannah was afraid if he didn't
slow down, he would have another one.

"Because if you'd like to go it alone, have me wait out here
for you...or just go on home...it's fine."

Hannah knew Joe was thinking this was a private matter,
and it would have been, had she not been so afraid of Gus's
reaction the first time he set eyes on Isabella. Feigning more
courage than she felt, she quipped, "Actually, Joe, I could use
a human shield right about now."

And like it or not, since the store had closed an hour before,
Joe was likely it.

"So if you don't mind..."

"I'd be glad to assist you, ma'am." Joe tipped an imaginary
hat at her and got out from behind the wheel. He opened the
rear passenger door and waited while Hannah unbuckled the
straps keeping the sleeping Isabella in her car seat. Carefully,
she handed her daughter over to Joe. Then she climbed out
on stiff legs.

She felt awful and exhausted, after the twenty-six hours in
the air, two standing in line in immigration, and another four
in the car. But this had to be done.

"Relax. It's going to be fine." Joe carried Isabella as far as
the front door.

Savoring his reassurance, even if she didn't quite believe
it, Hannah unlocked the door and pocketed her store keys.
"Keep saying that," she murmured as he handed the now-
stirring Isabella back to her.

Joe held the door open and Hannah squared her shoulders.
Plastering a smile on her face, she marched on through. Gus
was on a metal stocking ladder at the rear of the store, placing

stadium blankets on cubbyhole shelves just beneath the ceiling. "Dad?"

He turned. The expression on his face was wary rather than welcoming. Her heart sank.

"Hannah," Gus greeted her curtly.

Resentment and sorrow mingled inside of her. Stronger than that, however, was her determination to make this right. Isabella had come a long way. She had been through a lot. She deserved a better greeting from the only grandfather she was ever going to have. Hannah worked to keep her tone cordial. "Come down and meet your new granddaughter."

Gus plucked another blanket off the platform on the back of the stocking ladder. He turned his back to them. "Can't right now. I'm busy."

He wasn't doing anything that couldn't wait, she thought furiously.

Joe's brow furrowed, but he said nothing.

In Hannah's arms, Isabella stirred. Eyes still closed, she opened her cherubic mouth in a sweet, drowsy yawn.

Her father missed that. He was missing everything. Hannah's temper began to boil.

Damn it, this was an important day in her life and her father was ruining it by acting like a stubborn old fool!

Ever so gently, she transferred her baby to Joe.

Hands knotted at her sides, she walked to the rear of the store, got a second stocking ladder, and wheeled the twenty-foot apparatus over to the other. Deliberately, she turned it so it faced his. Her emotions still soaring, she began climbing.

Her father's frown deepened with every step she climbed. A mixture of disapproval and resentment tugged his lips into a frown. "Hannah, I do not have time to quarrel with you. I've got work to do this evening."

Too late, Hannah realized this was a showdown she should have had with her dad before she left. Instead of just waiting and hoping he would mellow over time. She stopped when she was at eye level with him. "Tough. This once, Dad, you're going to hear me out."

Gus shot a look at Joe who was standing a good twenty feet away, Isabella snuggled in his arms, then turned back to Hannah. Gus's expression remained grim as he warned, "We can do this later, young woman! In private."

She had never really stood up to her dad—until now. "We'll do it now." She matched his contentious tone.

He blinked. Obviously stunned, he demanded, "What's gotten into you?"

Tears stung Hannah's eyes. "I'll tell you what's gotten into me. The same thing that used to get into Mom when you were out of line with me!" Only now her mom wasn't here to play peacemaker and convince her father that what Hannah wanted—needed—wasn't so outrageous after all.

If she wanted him to understand her, support her, she was going to have to persuade him to do so herself. And that meant talking with him, even when he was like this!

Sighing, Hannah gripped the sides of the stocking ladder and continued, emotionally, "I love you, Dad. More than I can say. But I am not—I repeat *not*—going to let you disrespect my child."

Gus looked shocked. "Is that what you think I'm doing?"

"I don't know what you're doing!" Hannah paused as she saw him reach into his shirt pocket and then clutch his chest, as if in pain. "Dad!" Hannah cried.

Too late. He had already pitched to the left and lost his footing. Arms flailing, he fell sideways.

Helpless to do anything to prevent his swift awkward descent, Hannah watched in terror. Only later did she realize that the scream she heard as Gus slammed into a display of flannel shirts and jeans, was her own.

Chapter Four

The next half hour passed in a blur. There was a lot of swearing—from Gus. A lot of apologizing—from her—and a lot of calm reassurance to both of them from Joe. He also returned to baby duty, as Hannah knelt beside her father and fretted while the emergency medical technicians did their job.

Frustrated because she was not allowed to ride in the ambulance, Hannah climbed in the rear seat of Joe's Land Rover, next to Isabella's car seat. "This is all my fault," she said miserably. "I shouldn't have been arguing with my father."

Joe repeated what her father had already said half a dozen times. "It was an accident, Hannah. Accidents happen. Although if you want my two cents, your father shouldn't have been up on that stocking ladder in the first place. Work like that should be done by someone much younger."

Her fingers shook as she fastened her seat belt. "Easier said than done, unless we want to hire high-school students."

He caught her glance in the rearview mirror. "So hire high-school students."

How Isabella could continue to sleep through all the commotion, Hannah did not know. She sighed, and in answer to

Joe's question, said, "My father doesn't want kids that young at the Mercantile."

Joe steered his SUV into the hospital parking lot and parked in the slots reserved for the E.R. patients. "Well, maybe now is the time to change his mind."

Hannah knew something had to be done. Her father simply could not keep working at the rate he had been. He needed to relax and enjoy life. "You don't have to stay," she told Joe as she got out of the car and bent to remove Isabella.

He looked undeterred. "You may need my help."

It would be so easy to depend on him, so easy to fall for him. Hannah looked deep into his eyes. "Joe—"

He silenced her by pressing his finger to her lips. "There's nowhere else I'd rather be."

That quickly, the matter was settled.

"YOU'RE LUCKY THE CLOTHING display broke your fall," the emergency room physician, Thad Garner, said an hour later after all the tests had been done. Hannah had been called in from the waiting room to see her dad and hear the results along with him. "Otherwise," Thad continued with his usual bluntness, "you'd have more than a partially separated shoulder and broken arm."

Sweat beaded Gus's forehead and dampened his white hair. His skin was pale beneath the trademark scowl. "And now for the good news?" he grumbled, looking at Thad as if he were still the same kid who had stopped by the Mercantile to buy chewing gum after school.

"Surgery will be done first thing tomorrow morning, by the orthopedic team. Until then we'll move you to a private room upstairs and keep you comfortable."

Hannah could see the intravenous painkillers had already

eased her father's discomfort greatly. His irascible temperament was something else entirely. "Did he mention he was having chest pains when he fell?" She paced worriedly, not sure whether she wanted to hug her father or wring his fool neck.

"His heart is fine. For now. He still has to slow down. Stop working full-time at the store."

Gus moved as if to sit up and stomp right out of there, then fell back with a groan. "You doctors don't know what you're talking about." He winced and rubbed at the splint.

"I'm sure you think that, Mr. Callahan." The doctor flashed an amused smile, as the nurse packed ice around Gus's shoulder and arm. "In the meantime, we want you to get some sleep. So I'd advise you, Hannah, to go home and get some rest, too."

"Do you know what time the surgery will be?" Hannah asked.

The nurse piped up. "Seven-thirty tomorrow morning. If you get here a little earlier, you'll be able to sit with him before we take him up to the O.R."

Hannah thanked her for the information, then turned to her father. "Can I get you anything before I leave?"

Gus grimaced and turned his gaze away.

Hannah kissed his temple, anyway. "I'll be back tomorrow, Dad. Call the house if you need anything."

He muttered something she was just as glad not to catch.

Hannah slipped out of the room as the orderlies came in. By the time she reached the waiting area, where Joe walked back and forth with Isabella, her father's gurney had already been loaded onto the elevator.

"Everything okay?" Joe asked.

With Isabella cradled against his broad chest, he was the picture of a strong loving father. Hannah pushed the notion away. She could not afford to be overly emotional here. And she definitely could not afford to start fantasizing about things that were never going to be, no matter how attainable they seemed at this very moment. For Isabella's sake—as well as her own—if she were to ever get intimately involved with a man again, she and he would definitely need to be on the same page in terms of their futures.

Aware Joe was still waiting for an answer to his question, Hannah quipped, "Nothing a personality transplant wouldn't cure."

He chuckled. "I take it he's spending the night here?"

Hannah nodded and filled Joe in.

He looked as relieved as she felt that the injuries hadn't been any worse. Seeming to realize how much she needed a hug, he wrapped his arm around her shoulder and tucked her in close to his side. "I'll drive you two home," he murmured.

MINUTES LATER, HANNAH UNLOCKED the front door to the home she now shared with her father... "I can't believe she's still asleep," Hannah whispered, with a glance at the infant cradled against her chest. Isabella had fallen asleep in the hospital waiting room and hadn't stirred since.

Joe lugged her suitcase into the front hall and set it down. "I can't believe we're not," he joked.

Hannah turned to Joe. Although still as handsome as ever, there were shadows beneath his dark-green eyes and day-and-a-half stubble of beard on his face. He looked, just as she felt, in need of a hot shower and a bed before he gave in to fatigue and collapsed where he stood.

Slipping off her shoes, she padded soundlessly up the stairs and into the nursery that adjoined her bedroom. After brushing a gentle kiss across the baby's cheek, she lowered Isabella into the crib she had ready and waiting.

Joe lounged in the door, ready to assist, as she eased open the snaps of Isabella's traveling outfit, put on a fresh diaper and closed it back up. She covered her precious baby girl with a blanket. Joe moved to stand beside her, admiring the sweet picture of Isabella sleeping. With a sigh of contentment, Hannah switched on the nightlight, turned off the others and eased from the room. As they headed back into the hall, she faced him.

"You look like you're about to pass out you're so tired," she observed, knowing the cabin he was renting was another thirty minutes from there, on winding mountain roads that could be treacherous under the best of circumstances. "You probably shouldn't drive any more this evening."

One corner of Joe's mouth curved upward. Apparently amused at the way she was fussing over him, he inclined his head to one side and said drolly, "You're probably right about that, but it's too far to walk."

That quickly, Hannah's mind was made up. She took his arm in hand and led him farther down the upstairs hall. "You should sleep here tonight. You can stay in the guest room."

The laughter left his eyes. "You wouldn't mind?" he asked, searching her face.

She shrugged as if it was no big deal, when in fact it felt like a very big deal to her. She hadn't had a man sleep over in ages, for any reason, no matter how pedantic. And never here, in her childhood home. "Seems to me I owe you," she stated casually. And it was true. What was one night of hospitality after all he had done for her and Isabella over the past week?

Joe's gaze locked with hers, and a whisper of awareness slipped through her. "The pleasure of the past few days was all mine," he told her huskily.

And then he did what she was certain he had wanted to do for days. He took her in his arms and fit his lips over hers.

Hannah had been waiting forever for this, and he did not disappoint. The feel of his mouth against hers was electric. He tasted like mint and coffee...and man. Pressed up against hers, his body felt warm and solid and strong, his enveloping arms as seductive and tender as she ever could have wanted. As the contact continued, gently at first, then with intensifying passion, her emotions soared. He was everything she had ever wanted in a man. She felt a connection to him unlike any she had ever experienced, a longing that went soul deep. When he finally let the kiss draw to a close, she was so aroused she could barely breathe.

She started to speak.

Joe kissed her again, cutting off the need to somehow put a label on what had just happened between them. And this time when the kiss ended, he caught her by the shoulders and guided her to the bedroom that was hers. He looked down at her one long, last time. "Sweet dreams," he said. And then, hand to her shoulder, he guided her into the safety of her bedroom and shut the door between them.

"STOP HANGING AROUND this dang hospital and get yourself over to the Mercantile," Gus grumbled the moment he was out of the recovery room and ensconced in a private room the next morning.

"Dad, I want to be here," Hannah said patiently, glad Joe had kept the now-wide-awake Isabella Zhu Ming out in the waiting area, so her first impression of her grandfather wouldn't be as an impossibly grumpy old goat.

"And I want you at the store so I can stop worrying and go back to sleep," her father insisted.

The nurse adjusting Gus's IV looked at Hannah. "Your father is right. He's probably going to sleep the rest of the day. He'll rest more if you're not here."

Hannah hesitated.

"I promise you," the nurse said, steering her toward the door, as surely as Joe had steered her into the safety of her bedroom the evening before, "if there's any problem whatsoever—or if your father changes his mind and decides he wants you here—we'll let you know immediately."

Gus opened one eye. "I'm not changing my mind. I want peace and quiet!" he barked.

Hannah returned to her father's side and bent to kiss her dad's brow. "I'll be back this evening," she promised.

She slipped out of the hospital room.

Joe watched her approach expectantly when she met up with him and Isabella in the waiting room. If he were having second thoughts about the kiss they had shared the evening before, he was not showing it. Rather, the way he kept looking at her, when he thought she was distracted, said he wanted nothing more than to take her in his arms and do it again. Hannah knew exactly how he felt. She wanted to kiss him again, too. When she wasn't jet-lagged and emotionally vulnerable or upset about the actions of her cantankerous dad!

"How's your dad doing?" Joe asked in an intimate tone that was a balm to her ravaged nerves.

Hannah rolled her eyes in exasperation. "Well. Let's put it this way," she drawled, attempting to find the humor in the situation. "If grumpiness is a sign of a healing patient, he is definitely on the mend. Unfortunately, he's grumpy all the time and has been since my mom died."

"Before that...?"

She hesitated. "He's always been an exacting man. The thing is I know he was always harder on himself than he ever was on me and my mom." And that made his actions more understandable.

Joe fell in step beside her. "Was he that short-tempered with your mom?"

Hannah moved close to him to avoid a patient on a gurney. Their arms brushed and a tingle went through her. "Oh, no." Reddening self-consciously, she stepped away from him. Embarrassed about the swiftness of her reaction to him, she kept her gaze straight ahead. "My mom was the one person who could go toe to toe with him and if not come out the winner, end up in a dead heat with him. He listened to her about fifty percent of the time, and she listened to him about fifty percent of the time."

Joe shifted Isabella to his left arm and punched the down button on the elevator. He sent her another sidelong glance. "And you…?"

Hannah shrugged and stepped into the elevator ahead of him. "Wore a flak jacket—figuratively speaking—when things weren't going as my dad wanted. It was good training, though." She leaned against the opposite wall as the doors shut, once again leaving the three of them alone.

Trying not to notice how content Isabella looked cuddled up against Joe's chest, Hannah continued to recall. "By the time I headed off into the world to consult with clients about revamping the marketing plans for their businesses, I could handle even the most difficult personality and not take it personally."

Isabella leaned back abruptly and lifted a tiny hand to rub across the line of Joe's now routinely clean-shaven jaw. Hannah watched as Joe caught Isabella's hand in his much larger one and pressed a kiss to her closing fist. It amazed her to see how quickly her daughter was falling for Joe, too. Wordlessly "drafting" him to the daddy-figure in her life. Part of it, of course, was the fact he spoke the language Isabella had grown up hearing. The rest was simply…Joe.

Ruefully, he mused, "I'm guessing it's not easy to tell a customer their advertising is the pits."

Hannah nodded as the doors slid open. She preceded Joe out of the elevator, speaking over her shoulder. "Especially when the customer is a small business owner who's designed the failing plan themselves. They tend to take even the smallest suggestion for improvement very personally."

Joe fell into step beside her as they moved through the lobby. "And yet, from what I've heard around town, you were very successful," he said, pausing momentarily for the automatic glass doors to open.

"Because persistence usually pays off." Hannah walked out into the morning sunshine. The Texas sky was bright and blue, not a cloud in sight. Already warm, it was shaping up to be a beautiful August day. A harbinger for her life?

"Although I don't know if that's a technique that's going to work on my dad."

As they neared Hannah's minivan and Joe's Land Rover, which were parked side by side in the lot, Joe shifted Isabella to Hannah. "I'm sure you'll find a way to get through to him."

Hannah buried her face in the sweet-smelling hair on her daughter's head. "I hope so." Because she didn't think she could bear it if her and her dad's relationship continued on in this highly contentious way.

"OH MY WORD, SHE IS THE MOST adorable baby I have ever seen!" Ruthann Wilson said the moment Hannah walked into the Mercantile with Isabella and Joe, who was carrying the assorted baby gear Hannah needed to have with her at work.

Hannah grinned. Ruthann's reaction was exactly the one Hannah's mother would have given, had Izzie Callahan still been alive. And with good reason. She had not just worked at the Mercantile since Hannah was a baby, Ruthann had been her mother's best friend and the two had reared their children together. Although Ruthann's offspring were now happily married and living on the East and West coasts, Ruthann remained in Summit, two years after her own husband had died. She showed no signs of moving.

"Do you think she would mind if I held her?" Ruthann asked.

"Only one way to find out." Hannah gently passed Isabella to Ruthann.

Isabella let out a wail.

"Guess she's not ready for that." Ruthann handed her back to Hannah.

Isabella clung to Hannah's white linen blouse with both hands and looked around uneasily.

Seeing she was about to erupt in tears again, Joe spoke a few words in Mandarin Chinese. Isabella's tiny body relaxed.

Ruthann looked on approvingly.

"So how is that old rascal faring?" Ruthann asked eventually. "I take it he aced his surgery."

Hannah walked back to the glass-walled business office at the rear of the store. "Of course. Although I can't say the surgeons did much to improve his mood."

Ruthann chuckled as the front doors opened and a stream of people walked in. A tour bus was parked out front. A group of visitors filled the store aisles. Hannah looked around and saw only Marcy Nash at the cash register. Plus, the glass-fronted refrigerator that held the bottled water, lemonade and iced tea was nearly empty. That should have been stocked the previous evening, Hannah noted with dismay.

"Where's Buck Purvin?" Hannah asked as one of the

tourists turned up her nose at the oversize stainless steel percolator on the "free coffee" table.

Ruthann helped Hannah fit a cushioned canvas baby carrier over her shoulders. Hannah tucked Isabella inside and felt the infant relax even more, as she rested her face against Hannah's chest. "He broke his ankle trying to tame a rodeo bronc he bought for cheap," Ruthann replied.

Hannah frowned. That sounded just like Buck. He was always taking on more than he could handle when it came to horses, and just as frequently getting hurt.

"And Monte went back to college last week. So I had to send Luis to the feed warehouse to help out Jim, and with your dad in the hospital, that leaves only me, you and Marcy to mind the store."

"We can't possibly handle this many customers with just the three of us," Hannah insisted.

"Exactly why I've been trying to get your dad to hire another two full-time employees."

"And…?"

"He says he can't do it financially."

Hannah's brow furrowed. The store had plenty of traffic. Tourists flocked to the store year-round.

"Meantime, we've got a problem with this morning's delivery," Ruthann warned over her shoulder, pointing to the storeroom.

"Well, it's going to have to wait." Hannah walked out to wait on customers.

Forty minutes later, the group had purchased two thousand dollars worth of merchandise. The tour bus was on its way.

Joe was standing at the front of the store, chatting with a vacationing family from Maine about their favorite tourist spots in Texas, thus far, and offering them tips for the rest of their trip. They thanked him heartily and left, looking happy they had stopped in.

Hannah looked at the empty shelves on the snack foods aisle, then back at him. To her pleasure he seemed in no more hurry to move on than she was to see him leave. She squinted at him playfully. "How are you at shelving trail mix?"

He grinned, as ready to pitch in and help her out as ever. "I thought you'd never ask...."

JOE NOT ONLY SHELVED TRAIL MIX, beef jerky and freeze-dried camping foods, Hannah noted with satisfaction over the next hour and a half, he filled the refrigerator cases with bottled drinks and individually packaged ice cream treats. He also directed incoming tourists to the aisle containing whatever they wanted, while Marcy went to lunch and Ruthann ran the cash register.

Satisfied all was calm, for the moment, anyway, Hannah gave Isabella a bottle and a clean diaper, then went to the storeroom to investigate. She had only to walk in to see the problem Ruthann had mentioned.

She was still staring at the cases in astonishment when Joe came in to stand beside her. "What's going on?"

Hannah gestured to the towering stack of cardboard. "We've got two hundred cases of campfire beans here. We appear to be completely out of sodas. There's an oversupply of saddle cream, and way too many Western boots in ladies' sizes five-and-a-half and ten, and nothing at all in the more common sizes of six-and-a-half to eight."

Ruthann joined them.

"What happened to Dad's ordering system?" Hannah asked, nonplussed. She knew it wasn't computerized yet, but the mysterious method he used had always been very efficient.

Of course, Hannah knew inventory moved especially quickly in the summer, when lots of families came through Summit on the way to the Texas Rockies and Big Bend National Park. Still, in all her years working the store she had never seen a catastrophe like this happen.

Keeping one eye on the checkout stand, Ruthann shrugged. "There isn't one, at least not the way you think."

Hannah turned Isabella so she had a better view of her surroundings. "There must be," she protested.

Ruthann's lips tightened. "Let me rephrase. Gus has an ordering system, but it's in his head, and lately his memory hasn't been all that great. Hence, all the campfire beans. He kept thinking he forgot to order them and reordered them again and again over a period of a few days after you left for Taiwan."

Another wave of guilt flooded Hannah. Her becoming a single mom via adoption was causing her father so much stress. Yet she did not for one second regret adopting this wonderful little baby cuddled against her chest. What she did regret was the small amount of attention she'd paid to her father's managerial activities during the past six months.

"Between you and me," Ruthann continued, "I think he's overwhelmed since coming back from his heart attack last winter."

Ruthann's late husband had suffered from a heart condition, too, so she was proving to be an invaluable support system for Hannah and her father.

Hannah paused. "Is this forgetfulness something that will correct itself over time?"

Seeing a customer come in, Ruthann headed toward the

front of the store. "You'll have to ask his doctor that," she advised over her shoulder. "In the meantime, I think you might want to consider taking over at least this part of the business for him."

It was a good idea, Hannah thought. But convincing her father to let her do it would not be easy.

SINCE THE REST OF THE AFTERNOON was just as busy, Joe stayed around to help. Hannah felt both guilty and grateful for his assistance. She'd spent her entire adult life honing her independence. Yet she was now depending on Joe more and more. Not smart, given the fact he would soon be leaving.

At six-thirty when they closed up, Hannah turned to Joe and attempted to reestablish some boundaries. "I've got to pay you something," she began.

Joe ended the awkward moment with a single look. "Your money is no good with me," he said firmly.

In fact, Hannah noted uncomfortably, Joe looked slightly insulted she had even offered to compensate him. Which was understandable, she guessed, since he clearly made a lot more as an author than the staff employees at the Mercantile.

Hannah looked down at Isabella, who seemed to be tiring of the baby carrier. "Well, I have to say thank-you somehow." One hand cupped around Isabella, Hannah lowered the padded straps off her shoulders.

Joe stepped in to assist, his warm hands brushing her arm, as he eased the straps down, over her wrist. "You any good at proofreading?"

The warmth inside her increased. "I think so. Yes."

Joe caught Isabella beneath the arms, while Hannah lifted her out of the seat of the canvas baby carrier. "Then you can pay me back by reading the pages of my manuscript and hunting for typos and inconsistencies."

Hannah collapsed the baby carrier and put it aside. "Don't you have a spell-check function on your system?" she asked.

Joe's dark-green eyes bore into hers. "It doesn't catch every error. And it can't point out sentences that are confusing."

He struck her as being able to do that on his own. Still, she didn't mind an excuse to spend more time with him. And if it helped him even half as much as he'd been helping her… "You're on. I'll have to do it in the evenings, though," she cautioned. "And you might have to handle some baby-holding while I read."

Joe cuddled Isabella against his chest, seeming in no hurry to hand her back to Hannah. "I can handle that."

He certainly could. In fact, he looked as if he enjoyed spending time with Isabella every bit as much as Hannah did. Would he miss Isabella when he left? she wondered. *Will he miss me, as much as I'm going to miss him?*

She cleared her throat. "Speaking of cuddling…would you mind holding her a while longer while I close up the cash register? Ruthann is sweeping up the front."

"Sure thing," Joe replied. He carried Isabella over to the storefront to look at the storm clouds gathering on the horizon. "Looks like it's going to rain," he murmured.

"I hope it does. We need the rain." Hannah took the day's receipts and all the cash from the register, and carried them back to the safe in the office. She locked it up, then came back out. Joe was dancing Isabella around the store, murmuring to her in singsongy Mandarin. She wasn't smiling. Not yet. But she looked as close to blissful as Hannah had seen her thus far. Joy bubbled up inside her. She started toward them, then stopped as a young woman with hair the burnished-gold color of Joe's waved at them from the other side of the glass front door.

Grinning, Joe strode over to let her in. "Valerie!" he said as a wet gust of wind blew through the store.

"Hey, cuz!" She stood on tiptoe to buss his cheek, then drew back and looked him up and down, taking in the green canvas Callahan Mercantile & Feed apron and the remarkably content baby in his arms. "And I thought my life was the only one that had taken an unexpected turn!" Valerie drawled.

Chapter Five

"It's not what it looks like," Joe declared.

"What do you think it looks like?" Valerie teased.

That he was somehow involved with Hannah's baby. Which he wasn't. He was just lending a helping hand.

Joe gave Isabella to Hannah before any more false assumptions could be reached. "Hannah, meet my cousin Valerie Daugherty. Valerie, Hannah Callahan, one of the Callahans who run this place, and her daughter, Isabella."

"Nice to meet you." Valerie shook Hannah's free hand and touched Isabella's tinier one. She turned back to Joe and eyed his Mercantile apron with obvious surprise. "So when did you start working here? And where've you been?"

"I don't work here. I was just helping out because Hannah's dad had surgery today." Joe took the apron off and stuck it on the checkout counter next to the door. "And I've been traveling."

"According to the e-mail you sent Mom and Dad, you were supposed to be back from a trip yesterday afternoon. So I went to the cabin you rented. When you didn't show up by dark, I found out who the owner was and talked him into letting me in. Then I waited and waited, and you still didn't show up!" Valerie threw up her hands. "So where have you been?"

He was still contemplating how to answer that when Valerie looked at Hannah. "Oh," she said. "Oh!"

Now it really wasn't what his cousin was thinking.

"We were exhausted from all the traveling—and my dad's accident, shortly after we arrived," Hannah jumped in to explain. "Joe was too tired to drive out to the cabin so I insisted he stay in one of our guest rooms. And then he helped me out with Isabella while I was at the hospital during my dad's surgery this morning."

Ruthann's brow lifted in mute speculation.

"Aha!" Valerie said, concluding that he and Hannah had some thing going between them.

"There's no aha!" Joe said sternly, steering the conversation back to his cousin, whose problems were considerable, judging by her recent behavior. He leveled a lecturing finger her way. "And you could have called me to let me know you were here."

"I was trying to surprise you," Valerie said innocently.

He was surprised, all right. "Have you talked to your parents?" he asked.

Valerie's nose shot skyward. "Of course."

Uh-huh. And if he believed that, she probably had a hot stock tip for him, too. "When?" Joe demanded.

Valerie inspected an imaginary stain on the sleeve of her expensive and trendy blouse. "Maybe a week or so ago. Whenever they found out I wasn't at the university."

Joe curtailed his exasperation. "You need to call them."

Valerie's eyes narrowed. "You need to mind your own business."

Joe crossed his arms. "Hard to do when you show up on my doorstep and I know they're worried about you."

Valerie's lower lip shot out petulantly. "Are you going to let me bunk with you or not?"

"Only if you call them and let them know where you are."

"Forget that!" Valerie turned to Hannah, all sweet Texas charm. "Do you know where I could rent a room for this evening? All the hotels in town are full-up. I already checked."

To Joe's dissatisfaction, Hannah did not even look at him. "You can stay at my place," she said.

It was all Joe could do not to groan. "You don't have to do this," he said, looking deep into Hannah's eyes and telegraphing so much more.

To his frustration, Hannah deliberately ignored his message. "After all you've done for me and my family?" She radiated good cheer. "Really. I owe you. And this way," she continued in a voice rife with meaning, "you know Valerie will be safe."

"See?" Valerie said. "Everything is working out already. How much?"

Hannah held up a palm. "No payment is necessary."

Valerie's smile of cooperation turned into a scowl. "I wouldn't feel right imposing, unless we worked out a deal."

"Well..." Hannah shrugged. "I happen to know we're going to be shorthanded in the store tomorrow. Isabella has her first pediatrician's appointment—and with my dad already out...and tourists coming in by the busload..."

"Sounds like a fair trade." Valerie beamed.

Joe exhaled slowly. His aunt and uncle were going to blow a gasket over this.

"I'm going to call them and let them know you're okay," he told Valerie.

Valerie gestured carelessly. "Feel free. And pass on the message that I am not talking to them until they stop the inquisition about me leaving college."

"They might have a point, since you only have one year left before graduation."

"I'm not finishing my English lit degree." Valerie's tone took on that stubborn lilt he knew so well. "They need to get used to that."

The quarrel was interrupted when Isabella began to fuss.

Hannah paced back and forth, doing her best to comfort her child, as outside the gathering clouds darkened the sky even more.

The baby finally settled down again, snuggled closer and yawned.

"I was going to grab a quick bite and then go over to the hospital and check on my dad before I headed home," Hannah told everyone, gathering up the diaper bag and purse.

Ruthann interrupted. "There's no rush. You-all enjoy your meal. I'm going over to the hospital to see Gus, too, and I'll make sure he has everything he needs until you get there."

Hannah hedged, "I have to warn you—he's not in the best of moods."

Ruthann grinned. "So what's new? I reckon I've stood his crabbiness for the last thirty-five years, I can stand it for another evening."

Hannah looked relieved, and Joe could see why. Her father was ornery under the best of circumstances, coming out of anesthesia, laid-up and in pain, he was likely to be in wounded bear mode. As much as Hannah wanted to be there for Gus, she didn't want to put her baby in the line of the old man's fire. At least not until he'd calmed down about the whole adoption business.

Hannah turned back to Valerie, already acting more like an older sibling than Valerie's two overachieving brothers ever had, Joe noted, with pleasure.

"You're welcome to join me and Isabella for dinner," Hannah said.

"Hey…don't forget about me," Joe teased.

Hannah turned to him, obviously pleased he had extended their time together yet again.

Realizing his desire to be with her was getting stronger every day, he cast a look out the window. "I'll let you two work out the specifics about dinner, but you better hurry because that storm looks like it will be here before we know it."

JOE'S PREDICTION WAS RIGHT, Hannah noted. By the time they all got in her minivan and headed to a restaurant on the opposite side of town, rain was coming down in thick heavy sheets. She hated to emerge from behind the wheel. Plus, Isabella—exhausted no doubt from people fawning over her all day—had fallen asleep the moment they got her in the car seat.

"Plan B?" Joe said.

"How about you and I change places?" she asked Joe.

"Sure. I don't mind driving."

So far, so good. "How do you two feel about dropping me at the hospital so I can check on my dad while one of you stays in the minivan with Isabella. The other can zip in to get take-out dinners for us—on me. Then we can go back to my house and eat our take-out there."

"What about our cars?" Valerie asked.

"We can stop by the Mercantile and pick them up en route to the house," Hannah assured her.

"Sounds good to me," Valerie said, studying the front of the most popular steak place in the county. "Especially since it looks like there is quite a wait for tables judging by the people flowing out the door. How about I run in and get the dinners? Do you need me to get a menu for you two first?"

Hannah shook her head. "I've eaten here so many times I know it by heart."

"Same here," Joe said.

After they placed their orders with Valerie, she hopped out in the still-pouring rain. Isabella slept on. Joe and Hannah changed places and he drove Hannah to the covered portico at the hospital E.R. entrance. "He'll probably kick me out after fifteen minutes," Hannah warned.

Joe grinned. "If you make it that long."

Hannah agreed. She took one last loving look at Isabella, marveling at the treasure that was now hers to love and care for, and got out. She hurried through the hospital, her boots clicking on the shiny linoleum floors.

The halls were filled with soft laughter and the voices of visitors, cheering up patients. As she reached her father's room, Hannah braced herself and went in.

Ruthann was there, as promised. Fussing over Gus. Filling his glass with ice water from the plastic pitcher, fluffing the pillow behind his head.

Instead of resenting the attention, her father looked almost...grateful.

Hannah stared at the two in shock. She hadn't seen her dad so at ease since her mother died.

And she hadn't ever seen Ruthann and her father interact that way at the Mercantile.

She cleared her throat.

Ruthann flushed slightly and stepped away from Gus's hospital bed. "I didn't expect to see you so soon," she said.

Gus turned his head. It was clear the effects of the anesthesia he'd had that morning had worn off. And although he had a morphine pump beside the bed, he looked as if he hadn't used it much.

Curious, he asked with a harrumph, "Where's...?"

"Isabella?" Hannah asked.

Gus didn't exactly nod in acknowledgment. But he didn't turn away, either.

"I wouldn't have figured you'd get a babysitter already," he grumbled.

Hannah's mother had carried Hannah around in her arms, and in the kind of baby backpack that had been popular at the time. They had dozens of pictures of Hannah, happily nestled in her mother's arms or resting with her head on her mother's shoulders.

Lots of pictures of her with her dad, too. All of them unbearably tender, and happy and loving.

So Hannah knew Gus had it in him to be a great grandfather. When he decided to do that. She smiled and said affably, "She isn't with a sitter. She's with Joe."

Gus took a moment to consider that. "And what is he to you? You still saying he's just a casual friend?"

Hannah flushed. What little mophine her father'd had was definitely loosening his tongue. "Yes, Dad," she said, knowing that after the kiss they had shared the previous night—and the way he had been there for her over the past week—that her words were not exactly true.

Joe Daugherty was more than a friend now.

And part of her wanted him to be even more than that.

AFTER THEY ATE, JOE STAYED at Hannah's long enough to assist with Isabella's bedtime routine and see that Valerie settled in. Finally, there was no more reason to stay. Especially when he knew how exhausting the last few days had been for Hannah.

Joe reluctantly said good-night to his cousin, and Hannah walked him out.

It was still raining, the night air moist and mountain-cool.

Along the street, lights burned in the windows of the big stately houses that comprised the oldest part of the historic town.

Hannah gauged the distance to his SUV, which was parked third in the driveway. "Want to borrow one of my umbrellas?"

"Nah. I'll be okay." Joe studied the pensive look on her face. It wasn't the first time he'd seen it this evening. He reached out and took her hand in his. "You worried about your dad?"

Hannah looked down at their entwined fingers, momentarily leaning into his touch before drawing away. "They asked me to be at the hospital early tomorrow morning to talk to the doctors. It must be serious."

Ignoring his instinct to take her in his arms and kiss her until her worry went away, he dropped his hold on her hand and stepped back. "They already said his heart was okay."

"I know."

Ignoring the silky spill of straight, dark hair over her shoulders, he asked, "But…?"

The golden highlights around her face shone in the lamplight. "I know Dad and I aren't on the best terms right now, but I don't know what I would do if anything happened to him." Her voice shook and she took a step closer, her eyes holding more emotion than ever before. "And it's clear from what I saw at the Mercantile today, that things aren't going as well with the business as they have in the past."

He took another look at the shadowy houses on the street. The soft sound of falling rain, combined with the way lights were flicking off in the surrounding houses, only added to the romantic allure of the evening. "You think the business is in trouble financially?"

"I don't know." Hannah backed up against the porch post, and stuffed her hands in her pockets. "I haven't looked at the books. Dad has always kept them. And knowing how sensitive he is

about running everything himself—until the day he actually
does step down and hand over the reins to me—I haven't asked.
But I'm thinking now might be a good time to insist."

"Gus isn't going to like that," he warned.

Hannah's expression sobered. "I know. Which is why I
haven't done it yet. Because I didn't want to upset him."

Joe could only imagine how hard it was to be caught in the
dichotomy of aging parent and baby, simultaneously trying
to care for them both. It was one problem he would never
have. However, that did not mean he couldn't assist her—
temporarily—once again. "What can I do to help?" he asked.

Hannah's lips curved in the soft smile he liked so much.
"Be my friend?" she murmured.

HANNAH SAW THE KISS COMING. She probably should have
avoided it, given how rapidly her feelings for Joe were growing.
Especially when she knew he was going to leave in a few days.
But the pressure of his mouth over hers was like a balm for everything she had been through. Her heart expanded with
intense emotions that she couldn't begin to define.

Standing on tiptoe, she circled her arms around Joe's neck
and pressed her body close to his. She kissed him back, with
all the impossible yearning that had built up during their days
and nights together. She reveled in the tenderness that was so
much a part of him and discovered anew the passion, knowing
the confidences they had exchanged were nothing compared
to the heat and intimacy of this encounter.

Joe heard a car drive past and knew he should probably call
a halt to the impetuous embrace before he made even more
of a spectacle of them both, but the opportunity to be close
like this to Hannah was impossible to resist.

He knew they wanted very different things out of life, but

right now, tonight, there was no place he would rather be than with her.

Finally, it became clear to both, by the pounding in their hearts and the straining of their bodies, that her front porch was no place for this interlude.

Besides, with Isabella and his cousin inside the house—and Gus in the hospital—he was taking advantage.

Brought up short by his conscience, he broke off the kiss.

Her misty look cut off any apology he was about to make.

She was just as caught up in the wonder of the moment as he. And she knew full well the risks involved in furthering their involvement under the circumstances. There would be no happily-ever-after for them. "I'm only going to be here for a few more days," he said. A week, at the very most.

That was not enough for a woman like Hannah. A woman like Hannah required commitment, and the kind of promises he knew himself too well to ever make.

Her cheeks flushed in a way that brought out the delicate bone structure of her pretty face. "I know." She splayed her hands across his chest, her fingers warm and gentle. "I don't care." She looked into his eyes intently.

Keeping his hands from pulling her close yet again required a serious burst of willpower. "Hannah..."

She wrapped her arms about his neck and went up on tiptoe. The softness of her breasts nestled against the hardness of his chest. "I want to spend time with you, Joe."

He wanted that, too.

"I know you're going to be leaving. I know all the reasons we shouldn't pursue this. But you make me feel so reckless, Joe." She smiled and kissed him again until his breathing became more labored and his blood ran hot in his veins. Saying to hell with restraint, he deepened the kiss deliberately, until her mouth softened under his and she made an unbelievably sexy little sound in the back of her throat.

He raised his head slowly and she gazed at him. "So reckless," she repeated softly. After a whispered good-night, she extricated herself from his arms and walked inside the house.

HANNAH STOOD ON THE OTHER SIDE of the front door, her lips still tingling from the heated caresses she and Joe had just exchanged. She couldn't believe she had just done that. Said that. Meant it. She had never had an impetuous affair in her life. The two times she had been involved with men had been serious, five-year-long involvements that had not ended in the marriage she'd wanted.

She knew those relationships had been wrong. So she didn't regret ending them. She knew she was going to be sad when Joe left. She would be even more disappointed if she didn't act on what she was feeling for him. Explore this passion...just a little.

He was part of her life now, even if it was only for a fleeting moment in time...and she planned to cherish every second of it.

Hannah went to sleep dreaming of Joe. And woke with Isabella looking for him.

He wasn't there, though, when she changed, fed and dressed Isabella, and got ready herself. He wasn't with her when she went to the hospital to talk with her father and his doctor during his morning rounds.

Her father of course remarked on his absence right away.

"No Joe this morning?"

"He has his own life to lead, Dad. Work to do. A cousin in town..."

"Mmm-hmm." Gus's gaze was sharp. "Where's the baby?"

"Isabella is at the nurses' station." The group of veteran health-care workers had somehow coaxed Isabella into allowing herself to be held by someone other than Hannah or Joe.

Hannah should have been happy about that step forward in Isabella's acclimation to her new life.

She wasn't.

Maybe because there was now one less reason for Joe to delay his departure from Summit…and her life.

Gus harrumphed and started to cross his arms. He stopped when he felt what was obvious pain in the shoulder and arm still encompassed in cast and sling. "What's she doing there?" he demanded grumpily.

"Being doted on. She's getting quite good at accepting compliments." Although she still hadn't smiled. And Hannah was a little worried about that. Shouldn't her baby have been smiling by now—at least once? Most of the time, anyway, unless she was wet or hungry, Isabella did seem content.

Gus hit the remote, and shut off the TV mounted to the wall. "Why didn't you bring her in?"

For heaven's sake! Talk about being damned if you do and damned if you don't! "I didn't want to upset you," Hannah explained a great deal more patiently than she felt.

Gus took the decaf coffee from his breakfast tray. "Why would that upset me?"

Hannah threw up her hands, making no effort to hide her exasperation. "Because you didn't want me to adopt?" she chided.

Gus scoffed. "You did it anyway."

"Yes. I did. And now she's here and I don't want her feelings hurt. So…"

Gus drained his mug, then added what was left in the little carafe, which turned out to be only a drop or two. He frowned as he drank that, anyway. "You should bring her in. I won't bark at her."

Hannah peered at her father closely, wondering if they had done that secret personality transplant while he was in the operating room. "You're serious."

He heaved a loud sigh and looked completely out of patience. "Serious enough to think about getting out of bed unless you go and get her."

Joy bubbled up inside Hannah, even as she demanded right back in the same highly irascible tone, "How much morphine have you had?"

"Not enough to forget how to get you back in-line," Gus told her. He made a shooing motion with his good hand. "Now scoot. I want to get this fool doctor-patient-family conference over with."

Hannah returned with the newest member of the Callahan clan as her father's surgeon, cardiologist and family doc came into the room. "I didn't know it was going to be everyone," Hannah said, cradling Isabella in her arms and beginning to worry again.

The trio of doctors motioned for her to have a seat in the chair opposite the bed while they all stood. "We're concerned that your recovery is going to be tougher on you than you-all may have anticipated. With your arm and shoulder out of commission it's going to be very hard for you to dress or bathe—since you can't get the cast wet. And of course all tasks like driving are out of the question until you are fully healed."

"I still have one good arm and shoulder," Gus protested. "I can work a steering wheel with that."

"No driving until we give you the all clear," the surgeon repeated, "and that won't happen until after the cast and sling come off and you've completed physical therapy to regain full use of the arm and shoulder."

"Then how am I going to get around?" Gus argued.

"Hitch rides," his family doc advised.

"I'll drive you wherever you want to go, whenever you want to go," Hannah inserted quickly.

Gus scowled, not liking that option one bit.

"Furthermore, you're obviously pushing way too hard," the cardiologist said. "Your cholesterol is up. You're working too many hours. And you are still recovering from your heart attack last winter." He paused to look at the other two doctors, gaining consensus. "We all think it's time you retire."

"Not gonna happen," Gus growled.

"At the very least take the next three months off—entirely," the cardiologist said.

He disagreed. "I can't do that."

"I'm certain Hannah can manage the Mercantile," his family doc soothed.

Gus's bushy white brows lowered. "She has a new baby in case you three fools haven't noticed."

"Hannah's been known to juggle a thing or two simultaneously," Gus's surgeon remarked.

"What we are telling you is that you either take time off, and do everything you need to do to heal, or your health problems are just going to continue to mount," the family doc said.

"And if that happens," Gus's cardiologist warned, "you can kiss any hope of being around long enough to see this pretty little granddaughter of yours grow up."

Chapter Six

"You heard the doctors, Dad."

Gus did not try to conceal his irritation. "I heard a lot of nonsense is what I heard."

Hannah edged closer to her father, determined to get through to him. "It's either follow their instructions while staying at home recuperating, or find yourself right back in the hospital. And I know you don't want that."

"What's your point?" he asked curtly.

Hannah cuddled Isabella closer to her chest, loving her sweet baby warmth, and the way she leaned into—instead of away from—her these days. Touch was the main way the two of them communicated so far, and the way Isabella Zhu Ming snuggled against her was filled with love and trust. "I want to take over the business. Run it. My way. You promised me the Mercantile would be mine someday, when you were ready to step down. It's why I came home to stay last spring. But since I've been here, you've only let me do assistant manager stuff, and barely that."

Gus watched Isabella latch on to the buttons on Hannah's blouse. Which was yet another step forward in her daughter's development, Hannah thought with pleasure. Each day she was exhibiting more and more curiosity and the will to explore, just a little. "That's because we've never had an assistant manager," Gus argued.

"Exactly." Hannah winced when Isabella's tiny hands moved to the ends of her hair. "You should have."

"And there's no clearly defined role for one."

Hannah untangled her hair from Isabella's fist and gave the child her keys to grasp instead. "That can be changed if only you'd be serious about accepting my help!"

Isabella tossed the keys to the floor.

"I don't need you bossing me around, young lady!"

Hannah huffed in frustration and bent to retrieve the keys. She gave Isabella the typewritten breakfast menu placard from her father's food tray. "Well, I do need you, Dad! I need you to support me the way you have every other time I've chased after a dream or a goal. I need you to be the strong supportive father I've always been able to lean on—at least until Mom died and you turned bitter and cranky."

Gus made a reproving face at Hannah.

She mocked it until his scowl disappeared and she turned serious once again, her voice gentling as she spoke. "I need you to help me bring up my daughter, Dad. She needs a strong male role model in her life. And she deserves a doting grandfather who will show her what strength, courage and kindness are all about."

Noting the way Isabella was now chewing on the paper, instead of just examining it in her hands, Gus quirked a brow, a glint of humor slipping into his eyes. "Are you sure you're talking about me?"

Hannah took the paper from her daughter and exchanged it for a soft leather sunglasses case from her purse. She had to remember to start carrying baby toys with her at all times!

With Isabella momentarily content, Hannah perched on the foot of Gus's hospital bed. "Look, Dad, I know you've been in a very bad mood ever since Mom died. I don't blame you...I miss her, too. More than I can say. But the two of us are still here. And now I've adopted Isabella and she's a part of our lives, too. And we have to figure out how the three of us are going to be the kind of family she deserves, the kind of family that you, me and Mom were when I was growing up."

Gus's eyes touched briefly on the child in Hannah's lap, before returning to Hannah's face. "You talk like the two of us stopped being family a couple of years ago," he scolded. "That's simply not true."

"Well, sometimes it has felt like it." Hannah stiffened. Gus sniffed and she drew a deep breath, trying again to reach him. "Dad, I love you and I'm worried about you, and most of all, I want you to get better. So please, I'm begging you to take the time off your doctors are prescribing." She caught Isabella just in time, as the child leaned over and grasped the pattern on the white thermal blanket on the bed.

Hannah put Isabella, tummy down, across her lap and rubbed the infant's back. She continued her conversation with her father. "Let me run the store for three months. At the end of that time, when your docs give you the green light, if you want to come back and take over, then that's fine. But if you do, be warned—I'm going to have to find something else to do. Because I can't keep filling such a small role at the Mercantile and be happy, career wise."

Isabella tried to mouth the fabric.

Hannah sat her back up on her lap, facing Gus.

Again, his gaze settled briefly on his new granddaughter before moving deliberately away. "You drive a hard bargain," he told Hannah.

She accepted the comment with a shrug. "Maybe because I learned from a master."

"All right." Gus tried but couldn't quite suppress a smile. "I'll let you run the store—your way—for two weeks."

Hannah's mouth dropped open. "Two weeks!"

"You can do anything you want," Gus continued, as authoritative as always, "but at the end of that time, if we don't see definite improvement, and I'm off all this dang pain medication and able to get around a little better, then I'm coming back to work."

"Eight weeks," she bartered.

"Six. Because that's when my cast comes off."

"Done." Hannah stood and they shook hands.

Gus looked at Isabella, stirring restlessly in Hannah's arms. Curious, he asked, "Don't you have a pediatrician appointment for her today?"

Glad her father was paying more attention to what was going on in her life than he let on, Hannah nodded. "In twenty minutes."

"Then you better get a move on," he advised, still evidencing no desire to hold his granddaughter. "Hadn't you?"

"HERE'S THE GOOD NEWS," Isabella's pediatrician, Sandra Carson, said cheerfully after giving the baby a thorough physical examination. "Isabella appears to be in pretty good health overall."

Hannah looked down at her daughter. Isabella had been quiet and cooperative until she'd had to undress down to her diaper and lie down on the exam table. That had scared her and made her cry. Eventually, Hannah and the blond fortysomething pediatrician, who was married and had two kids of her own, had been able to soothe Isabella into tranquility. She was now seated on Hannah's lap and looking off into space.

Seemingly unperturbed by the fact Isabella was now staring almost trancelike at the growth chart on the wall,

Sandra Carson continued going over her findings. "The bad news is that Isabella is underweight. And like most babies who have spent the majority of their first year of life in an orphanage, your daughter is lagging behind in most aspects of her development. At ten months, Isabella should be able to sit and pull herself up on her own. She should be crawling and eating both pureed and finger foods, in addition to the formula she consumes every day."

Hannah had worried about that, too.

Sandra opened up the cupboard above the sink and took out a handout entitled *Feeding Your Baby*. She gave it to Hannah to take home and read. "But don't worry. We'll have her caught up in no time. And of course if you have any questions about the feeding schedule we want you to follow, you can call the office and talk to the nurse."

"I will," Hannah promised.

Sandra looked at Isabella, who was now studying the window blinds with the same trancelike stare and continued, "Isabella is also going to need to have her vaccinations readministered, since they were done while she was in the orphanage and we can't be sure the medications were stored and administered properly. Sometimes, unfortunately, they're not. So just to be absolutely certain she is protected we will redo them. We're also going to have to take some blood so we can screen her for hepatitis, HIV, anemia and a few other things." Sandra sent a fond look at Isabella who was still focused on the slats of the window blinds and commented dryly, "Most infants aren't wild about this procedure. And last but not least we need to do a PPD test on her arm to test her for tuberculosis."

Feeling a little overwhelmed again, Hannah shifted Isabella on her lap. "That all has to be done today?" It seemed like an awful lot!

The pediatrician made a note on Isabella's chart. "The sooner we get it done, the better." Sandra paused to ruffle Isabella's hair, then smiled at Hannah. "Any questions before I send the nurse back in?"

Yes, Hannah thought, one very important one...

Feeling very much like a new mother, she asked nervously, "When do you think she might start smiling? I mean, there are times now when she seems content and she snuggles up close to me, but there are other times like right now when she's under stress, when I think she's going back into this other world, emotionally." Times when Isabella seemed light-years away.

Sandra turned to Isabella, who had gone back to staring stoically at the growth chart on the wall.

"That other world comforted her for a long time before you came along to give her a real home," Sandra said gently. "So much right now is new and completely unfamiliar to her, from the language spoken to the way people around here look, to the sounds and smells of the food and air around her. She's adjusting and will continue to adjust but it will be at her own pace."

"In other words," Hannah paraphrased, "don't worry. Relax. Let it happen naturally."

"Right. Which, by the way, is the advice I give all new parents, whether they've adopted or had their kids biologically. All the worrying means is...congratulations!" Sandra high-fived Hannah and grinned. "You're a parent!"

A parent, Hannah thought, who was happier and more challenged all the time. Now if the rest of her life could fall in line, even half as easily....

HANNAH HADN'T PROMISED TO CALL Joe to let him know how Isabella's pediatrician appointment went, nor had he asked her to do so, but he hoped to hear from her just the same.

When the phone rang, he picked up without bothering to check the caller ID screen—then immediately wished he had.

"We do not understand why you couldn't just get Valerie to head home," Aunt Camille told Joe.

"Surely she knows we're worried about her," Uncle Karl chimed in.

Joe hated these family conference calls. Hated being made to feel like he was somehow "less" a Daugherty than Karl and Camille's own children, yet again.

Joe rubbed the bridge of his nose. "She's not ready to talk to you."

"Well, since she's not returning our calls or talking to us we need you to tell her that we talked to the Dean of Students. He agreed to remove this unfortunate episode from her transcript entirely as long as she attends counseling sessions, either at the university or with a private therapist. She can go back to college in the fall and it will be like this minibreakdown of hers never happened!"

Buying a way out of trouble never solved anything. Unfortunately, it was the only solution Camille and Karl had. "Look, I know you're worried about her, but I have to tell you, Valerie seems fine to me." Ticked off about something, Joe added mentally, but fine.

"Well, obviously, Joe, she is not fine," Aunt Camille huffed, "or she would never have moved out of her dorm at the end of the summer term without finishing her classes!"

Joe shut his eyes in frustration. "This is between you and Valerie. You all need to work it out." *And leave me out of it,* he added silently.

"You're family, Joe," Uncle Karl persisted.

Sure. Now that it was convenient and they needed him to accomplish something for them, he was "family."

Joe paused. Tried again. "I'm sure she will get in touch with you soon. In the meantime she's here, staying with a friend of mine and her daughter and father. She's helping out at their store today. In a day or so, if no one tells her what to do, she may even head home on her own."

Aunt Camille cried, "We need this resolved now!"

"You're going to have to be patient." Joe talked a few more minutes, then hung up.

No sooner had he put down his cell phone, then it buzzed again. The caller ID said Summit Hospital. Wondering if this could be Hannah, Joe picked up. Braced for Hannah's voice, he was stunned to hear Gus on the other end of the line.

"OH, SWEETHEART," HANNAH soothed Isabella, cradling her in her arms and pacing across the living-room carpet, "I know you're having a tough time today." Hannah kissed the top of her fussing daughter's head. "But I promise you you're going to feel better just as soon as the acetaminophen kicks in."

Isabella responded by breaking into a loud wail.

And it was at that moment that Hannah heard the front door open behind her. Joe Daugherty stood in the portal, her dad leaning heavily on Joe's arm.

Isabella sobbed all the harder.

Her father's face was so pale he looked like he might faint right then and there.

Hannah shifted Isabella to her left arm, and rushed to offer what help she could. She held the door while the summer heat blew in. Joe guided her dad—whose gait was shaky to say the least—to the closest seat. Gus collapsed into it, grimacing when his injured arm and shoulder awkwardly brushed against the back of the upholstered chair.

Joe went back to bring in a bag and shut the front door.

Isabella stared at Joe, then began crying again, all the harder.

Joe comforted her in soft fluent Chinese. Isabella turned her face up to his. Hannah handed the baby over. "She's got a bottle in the warmer on the kitchen counter," she said. "It should be ready now."

Looking like he knew he had just been given the easier chore, Joe nodded and walked off, Isabella's wails diminishing only slightly.

Hannah turned back to her father, eyebrows raised. "What are you doing home?"

"I could ask the same question of you," Gus griped, acting as if he were the one who had the right to be exasperated. He leveled an accusing finger at her. "Aren't you supposed to be managing the Mercantile now?"

Hannah flushed, irked to find herself on the defensive, when it was Gus who should be explaining himself to her. "Isabella's running a fever in reaction to her immunizations. I had to bring her home."

He didn't argue with her assessment—they both knew a crying baby had no place in a business setting. He frowned and settled farther back in his chair. The slight movement made him wince in obvious pain. "Exactly the problem with you running the store, full-time," he groused.

Back to that? Next he'd be telling her she couldn't possibly run the store as a single working mom. "Isabella isn't going to be sick that often, Dad."

"You know how I feel. When the Mercantile is open for business, a Callahan should be there. Period."

"You also said, just the other day, that I shouldn't be leaving her with a sitter, just yet! So what, pray tell, am I supposed to do then?"

Joe walked back in, Isabella cradled in his strong arms.

Both hands wrapped around her bottle, she had her head turned toward Gus and Hannah.

She could have sworn Isabella was paying more attention to her dad than to her, but then her heart sank when Gus turned away from Isabella's winsome regard.

Joe noticed and stepped in to fill the void. "I think it's time for your dad's pain medication," he said. He shifted Isabella closer to his chest. The baby nestled against the broad strong surface exactly the way Hannah would have liked to do.

"The nurse said he should take it when he got home," Joe continued, nodding at the white pharmacy bag sticking out of the outside pocket on her dad's overnight case. "Not before, because it might make him a little woozy."

"It does make me woozy," Gus said flatly. "And I'm not taking it. I want my wits about me."

TO JOE'S EXASPERATION, Gus held out for another half hour. Then, sweaty and pale, he let Hannah talk him into taking one of the pills the hospital pharmacy had sent home with him.

Shortly thereafter, the old rascal was sleepy enough to let Joe help him upstairs to bed. It was a harder journey than either of them expected, with Joe taking on much of Gus's considerable weight as they moved slowly up the stairs and down the hall to the master bedroom.

"Does he want a cold drink up there?" Hannah asked when Joe joined her in the kitchen moments later.

Joe tried not to think how glad he was to see Hannah, or be there with her in an intimate setting again. He wasn't used to needing anyone in his life. Yet for reasons he couldn't quite fathom, he needed to see her and Isabella, to feel like his day was worth something.

Joe leaned against the kitchen counter, watching Hannah

move about the kitchen with the grace of a ballerina on stage. She had taken off her footwear, as was her habit, shortly after walking into the house, and put Isabella in a baby carrier that strapped across her chest. Isabella was asleep, with her head pressed against the pillowy softness of her mother's breasts. It looked, Joe thought, like a good place to be.

"Or something to eat?" Hannah persisted, still trying to figure out how to make her father comfortable.

Joe jerked himself out of his reverie. "Gus said no, to food and-or drink. He intends to sleep."

Hannah sighed and moved around the room, her socks padded across the wood floor. Her denim skirt, stopped at midcalf and swished around her legs. She'd swept her glossy hair into a clip on the back of her head, but a few strands escaped, falling over the band collar of the embroidered lawn blouse she wore over a white tank top.

Joe found himself wishing he could run his fingers through those errant strands. "But I'll take a tray up to him, anyway, if you'd like." Joe continued his efforts to be helpful.

"No." Hannah sighed, looking even more stressed. "I'll check on him in a few minutes. Right now I want to talk to you." She pointed to a kitchen chair.

Feeling the way he had when he was a kid and undeservedly got called to the principal's office, Joe sat.

Hannah set a glass of iced tea in front of him, and a plate of shortbread cookies on the center of the table, and settled opposite him. "How is it that you brought my dad home from the hospital?" she asked, looking a little confused and more than a little peeved.

Joe shrugged. "He called and asked."

"You," Hannah repeated, as if she were still having trouble believing that.

He knew how she felt. Initially, the request had come out of left field for him, too.

"He didn't want to bother you." He parroted the reason Gus had given him. "He said his friends are all his age and can't get off work this time of day. Unlike me. Who's a writer. And therefore doesn't work."

It was Hannah's turn to look as if she wanted to sink through the floor in embarrassment. "Tell me he didn't actually say that."

Joe merely smirked, enjoying the exchange more in retrospect than he had at the time. "Your dad also noted I seem to spend a lot of time gallivanting around, here and there. I mentioned that was research for my book, but he pointed out that I was able to go to Taiwan with you to get Isabella at the drop of a hat, so I can't be all that busy."

She buried her face in her hand. "I'm sooo sorry," she muttered.

Enjoying the flood of new color in her cheeks, Joe leaned back in his chair. "Don't you want to hear the rest?"

Hannah spread her fingers and peered out at him. "There's more?" she asked weakly.

"Oh, yes, and it's the good part." Joe regarded her steadily, wondering what her reaction to the next bit of news was going to be. "I agreed to stay here until your dad is steady enough to make it up and down the stairs and in and out of bed by himself. Gus wants me in the guest room next to his, with you, Isabella and Valerie all down at the other end of the hall."

Hannah blinked in astonishment and dropped her hand to her lap. "Why would you do that?" she asked.

Heck if I know, Joe thought. It wasn't like him to get involved in anyone else's problems. Yet, in the past few weeks, he had come to Hannah's and Isabella's—and now Gus's—rescue more times than he could count. "I figured I owed you, since you're giving my cousin a place to bunk and all."

"She's working that off at the Mercantile! And I owed you!"

"So now you'll owe me more," Joe joked.

Hannah's delectably soft lower lip slid into a pout. "Well, I don't know how it could get any worse," she complained.

Joe did.

With relish, he informed her. "Your dad has noticed the 'sparks' between us."

Hannah's cheeks went from pink to scarlet.

Joe couldn't help it—he grinned. Then he paused dramatically before dropping the bombshell. "And Gus wanted me to know that if I was interested, you were more in need of a husband than ever."

Chapter Seven

Hannah stared at Joe, still reeling from the revelation about her father's audacious matchmaking. Afraid her voice would rise and wake the baby, she stood and headed into the adjacent dining room. Aware of Joe's gaze on her, she carefully unhooked the thick straps and extricated Isabella from the carrier. Only when she had the baby settled in the wooden cradle she had used as a child, and covered with a fleecy pink blanket, did she return to the kitchen.

With a deep breath, she settled opposite him once again. "What did you say to him?" she asked, aware—without wanting to be—how right Joe looked sitting in her kitchen.

His lips curved into a smile. "The truth. That I'm not the marrying kind."

A wave of disappointment wafted through her. Hannah wrapped her hands around her glass of iced tea. She was almost afraid to ask. "And to that, my dad said?"

Joe shrugged and ate another cookie. "That neither was he, until he met your mother."

Hannah moaned in despair. She did know why she kept finding herself in these situations. Never mind why she felt so tied to Joe, a guy they both knew she had no business getting attached to. "I'll talk to him," she promised. "Although, I have to tell you, it probably won't do any good. I've asked my father not to meddle in my love life, or lack thereof, multiple times since I've been back in Summit."

Joe chuckled. "Gus doesn't listen?"

Hannah gave Joe her brightest smile and reached for a cookie. "He seems to—albeit reluctantly." Feeling a self-conscious warmth move from her chest into her neck, she paused. "I always think I've communicated my feelings and have gotten through to him, and then five minutes later I turn around and he's trying to set me up again. It's extremely frustrating."

Joe studied the ice in the bottom of his glass. "But not all that unusual, from what I've noticed. A lot of people have trouble talking to their parents."

Hannah grabbed the pitcher and refilled Joe's glass. "It's not just my dad. I've never been able to make the men in my life understand what I do and do not want from them, either."

Joe lifted a brow. She realized she had revealed more than she'd intended. "Go on," he said softly.

Heat moved from her throat to her cheeks. "It's nothing."

He looked at her over the rim of his glass. "It's something if you brought it up." He lowered his drink. "We're friends, Hannah. We can talk about this if you want."

Hannah knew she needed to unburden herself to someone. Joe was an articulate guy, who seemed to "get" her in a way no one else ever had. Maybe he could help her understand the male point of view in these situations. Certainly, it was worth a try. She swallowed and forged on. "I've been seriously involved twice. The first time was right after college, when I was just starting out in the business world. I really wanted to be successful. Mostly," she admitted with rueful honesty, "to prove my dad wrong."

Joe waited for her to continue. The compassion in his green eyes made it easy. "He thought the world of big business was no place for a woman, and that I should be spending all my energy looking for a husband capable of running the Mercantile for me, when the time came. My plan was to work for two years, get some experience and then enter business school and get my MBA."

Joe nodded approvingly. "Makes sense."

"Not to the guy I was involved with," Hannah reminisced. "Ron didn't want his 'woman' out-performing him. He pretty much told me that if I went to grad school at the same time he did, and pursued a high-powered career as a consultant, we were over. He wanted 'a wife,' not a competitor."

"Ouch."

Hannah sighed. "So of course we ended it. I took two years off from dating and went to Northwestern, got the great job that had me traveling all over the world. And got involved with the second guy. Barry was a former army medic who was just starting med school in Chicago. Same age as me. Very well-traveled, experienced, mature. Knew what he wanted. Didn't mind my devotion to my profession, or the fact I was on the road all the time because he was just as busy, learning how to be a doctor."

His gaze traveled over her lazily. "Sounds perfect."

"You'd think so, but Barry never understood how much I eventually wanted to get married, have kids, settle down. Still have a career but put family first."

He shook his head and helped himself to another cookie. "You didn't talk about this stuff?"

"We discussed it all the time," Hannah recalled wearily. "Barry just didn't think I was really serious. Turns out, he wanted to be married, but he didn't want kids or any kind of conventional life. Apparently, he thought, because of the way I worked, that I didn't, either…that it was all just talk. When he found out my wishes were sincere, he told me how he felt and we broke up." She sighed. "Then my mom died. I realized life was short and decided to heck with trying to find a man who wanted what I wanted when I wanted it, and decided to adopt. Halfway through that process, I came back to Texas, because my dad needed me. And I'm glad I'm here."

Joe pushed away from the table, and settled more firmly in the wooden Windsor chair, his hands resting on his spread thighs. "Just not glad he's meddling."

Trying not to think what it would feel like to sit on that lap of his, Hannah nodded. She returned her attention to his face. Locking gazes with him, she admitted, "And now I'm having the same problem with my dad that I had with Ron and Barry. He hears me. He just doesn't take me seriously."

Affection softened the ruggedly handsome lines of Joe's face. "I take you seriously."

Deliberately, Hannah reined in the ardent nature of her thoughts. "Which is great," she replied, knowing no one would protect her heart in a situation like this, but herself, "but you and I aren't involved nor are we likely to be given our different paths in life."

"True."

Hannah figured she'd had enough disappointment in the romance department, without inviting any more, no matter how daring Joe made her feel. "I'm making a life in Summit."

"And I'm leaving soon," Joe summed up the situation soberly.

"Right."

"So your dad can matchmake all he wants. It's not going to change anything."

Hannah nodded. They would continue to be friends who had kissed a time or two, and flirted with the notion of making love, but had never taken it any further. And it was good they hadn't, because if she had made love with Joe she might do something really foolish and fall in love with him.

Desire flared in Joe's eyes and, just as swiftly, disappeared. "So we're okay even if we never pursue this?" he asked quietly.

As much as we can be under the circumstances, given how much I want you and can never have you. At least not the way I want, Hannah thought. She stood and put her glass in the sink. "Yes. Although I still want to wring my dad's neck for sticking his nose in my business."

Joe shrugged off the paternal interference in his usual easygoing manner. "Gus had your best interests at heart."

Hannah wished she could be that accepting of Gus's bullheadedness. "He needs to find a better way to help me out," she insisted stubbornly.

"I'm sure he will, given a little more time, and a lot more reminding from you." Joe placed his empty glass next to hers. His body brushed hers inadvertently before moving away, with the same easy grace. "Anyway, if I'm going to bunk here for a few days to help your dad get around, as needed, I'm going to need to go back to my cabin and pick up some clothes and my laptop and printer."

Hannah thanked him for his continued help and walked him as far as the front door. She paused, her hand on the knob. "Just so you know, I haven't forgotten about the manuscript I promised to proofread for you."

Standing close, Joe spared her a kind glance. "Listen, it's okay if you bow out," he said, bending down to casually kiss her cheek.

The contact brought forth a flare of desire. Hannah turned toward him. For a second, she thought he was going to kiss her again, and knew she'd be lost if he did. Trembling, Hannah stepped back, cutting him off with a lifted hand. "There's no way I'm letting the giving in this situation be all on your part," she told him in a low voice. "I'll find the time." *And I'll work on curtailing my feelings.* "I promise."

BY THE TIME JOE GOT BACK TO the Callahan residence, it looked like a party was going on. Lights were blazing. Six cars crowded the driveway. More sat in front of the house and on the street. Joe parked as close as he could get, being careful not to block another neighbor's mailbox or driveway. Grabbing his stuff, he headed in.

Before he could ring the bell, the door swung open. Two couples—both looking to be in their early seventies—greeted Joe on their way out. Inside there were changes, too.

A "Welcome Home Isabella Zhu Ming Callahan!" banner was strung above the fireplace. Gaily wrapped presents were heaped on the coffee table. Hannah was sitting on the sofa, a wide-eyed Isabella in her arms. She was surrounded by women, all of whom were cooing over the baby. Gus was in his favorite club chair, surrounded by the men.

From time to time, Gus sneaked a peak at his new granddaughter, but his outward demeanor was cool, and he kept the conversation on the upcoming football season.

Joe knew everyone there. They were all longtime members of the community he had met while doing research on his book. There were also a few guys his own age, all of whom had designs on Hannah. Not that she'd seemed to give them any encouragement, so far as he could tell.

"Hey, cuz!" Valerie swept up to give him a hand, looking right at home on the couch beside Gus's friend Ruthann. "We're having a surprise party for Isabella and Hannah! Isn't it great?"

"I wish I'd known," Joe murmured, feeling a little like an outsider once again. "I would have brought a gift."

"I think everything you've done and are doing for them has been gift enough," Ruthann chided firmly.

He supposed that was true. Still, he didn't like being out of the loop, even inadvertently, and that went double where Hannah and Isabella were concerned...

"I've got a problem I need to talk to you about." Valerie took hold of his shirtsleeve. She steered him into the foyer, out the front door and onto the porch. "Chris Elliott has been talking to Mom and Dad and telling them that he thinks I've been having a nervous breakdown."

That was ridiculous, Joe thought. "Why would he say that?"

Her expression went from resentful to evasive in a millisecond. "I don't want to get into it."

Too bad, because I do, Joe thought. Knowing there had to be more behind her unusual actions than she had revealed so far, he probed. "Did you and Chris Elliott break up because you dropped out of college? Or did you drop out of college because the two of you broke up and you didn't want to be around him anymore?"

"The latter, of course." Valerie appeared insulted.

"Does he want you back?"

She propped both her hands on her hips. "What do you think?"

That you're still not telling me everything, Joe thought. In an effort to get his normally talkative cousin to confide in him, he observed, "It doesn't sound as if he's going about winning you back in a very logical way."

Valerie's jaw clenched. "Actually, it's extremely logical. Manipulative, even."

That clue was no help at all. Joe edged closer. "You want me to have a talk with him?" he asked.

Valerie scowled. "I want you to run interference, if he shows up here. I'm already embarrassed enough that I ever went out with him at all, never mind dated him for three years! I don't want him finding out I'm working at the Mercantile and showing up and creating a scene in front of everyone."

What was she talking about? "I thought you were only helping out temporarily," Joe said.

Valerie beamed. "I did so well this morning, Hannah offered me a full-time job—with benefits—if I want it. She also said I can bunk here, until I can get enough money together to rent a place of my own."

That was nice of Hannah, albeit misguided. "You don't want to try and transfer to another college for fall semester?" he asked.

Valerie's lower lip shot out. "Nope."

Joe raked his hands through his hair. "Your mom and dad are going to go nuts over that," he warned.

"Too bad. At this point, they are every bit as much a problem to me as Chris Elliott is."

"I'M REALLY EXCITED ABOUT ALL the changes you're going to make at the Mercantile," Valerie told Hannah as they were cleaning up.

Ruthann—who had put together the meal for the welcome home gala—sat in a rocking chair in the corner of the kitchen, gently lulling a drowsy and exhausted Isabella to sleep.

As Hannah looked over at her late mother's best friend, an

unexpected wave of poignancy spilled over her. She was happy Isabella was finally letting others hold her, but she wished her own mother were here to share this momentous time with her. It would have meant so much to both of them....

When a throat cleared in the doorway, the women turned in unison. Gus wavered unsteadily in the portal. Joe was at Gus's side, a hand beneath her father's elbow.

"What changes?" Gus demanded gruffly.

Clueless about his feelings toward change, particularly at the family store, Valerie gushed. "Hannah's putting in a really nice coffee bar with Starbucks-quality machines where that folding table with the old-fashioned coffee percolator is right now. In fact, she's rearranging the whole layout of the store."

Gus glared at Hannah. "A coffee b-bar?" he sputtered.

Arguing would get them nowhere. The proof, Hannah knew, would be in the sales at the end of the six-week period her father had agreed upon. "You gave me the authority to do whatever I deemed necessary to increase business, remember?"

Ruthann stood and walked over to Gus with Isabella still in her arms. "Let's you and I go sit on the living-room sofa. Shall we?"

Hannah thought her father was going to refuse, for a lot of reasons, the least of which was the infant in Ruthann's arms. It was clear, however, that her dad was in post-op pain. And all the moving around was only making it worse.

"I'll bring your glass of apple cider and your pain medicine to you," Joe said.

Gus nodded. Slowly, he turned and made his way back the way he had come, with Joe right behind him and Ruthann on his other side.

Hannah got out a tall glass, filled it with crushed iced from the fridge dispenser and got out the jug of cider. She barely had enough to fill the glass. Joe was back for the drink and a caplet from the prescription bottle.

"I'm going to have to go to the grocery for more cider," Hannah said. Whenever her father was sick, it was the one thing he wanted without fail. And it was an item not currently carried at the Mercantile.

"I'll go." Valerie grabbed her shoulder bag off the hook next to the back door. "What else do you need?"

Hannah wrote out a short list and handed Valerie some cash.

She could hear the sound of muted conversation coming from the living room. She started to peek around the corner, only to have her way blocked by Joe's tall muscular frame. "She's talking sense into him. I suggest, for all our sakes, you let her continue."

Hannah stepped back, the brisk masculine fragrance of his hair and skin filling her senses. "Isabella—"

"Is going to sleep in Ruthann's arms." Joe looked around the kitchen. He noticed the filled plastic trash bags next to the back door. "I'll take those out."

Sensing he wanted a chance to talk to her alone, Hannah added, "I'll help."

They each grabbed two sacks by the tie handle and walked through the back door into the cool summer night. "Where do you keep your can?" Joe asked.

"Next to the toolshed." Hannah led the way through the landscaped backyard to the big wheeled cart. She lifted the lid, and they dropped all four bags in.

She stood there, breathing in the cool night air. "Your dad will come around to the changes you want to make at the Mercantile," Joe said.

Hannah inhaled a long, slow breath. She turned and faced Joe, her heart racing at their proximity. "But will he come around to Isabella?" she asked quietly, wanting, needing the assurance only Joe seemed able to give.

He shrugged and stuck his hands into the pockets of his cargo pants. "He seems to be accepting her."

Not the way he should, Hannah thought resentfully. "He hasn't held her yet. Or spoken to her, or even taken her little hand in his." All things she would have expected a doting grandfather to do.

Joe clapped a reassuring hand on Hannah's shoulder. "He will. In time."

She swallowed, not so sure....

Joe put his other hand on Hannah and deliberately turned her to face him. He waited until their eyes met and held. His voice carried a deep, pleasing resonance. "She's impossible not to love."

Hannah's lower lip quivered at the tenderness in his touch. "What if...?" She stopped, unable to go on.

Joe's grip tightened protectively. "What?" he prodded.

She swallowed. "The stress of having her here, of me making changes at the Mercantile, are too much for my dad's heart...or somehow impede his post-op healing?"

Joe's hands slid down her arms. He took both her hands in his. "First of all, if you don't follow through with whatever ideas you have in mind for the business, the store is going to continue to decline. That will cause financial stress, which will definitely be bad for Gus's spirits and his heart. Second, scientists have proven that the act of petting a dog or cat can lower a person's blood pressure and stress. I'm fairly certain that holding a baby has a similar effect."

Hannah couldn't help it. She smiled. Her fingers entwined with Joe's. "I do feel pretty relaxed whenever I'm rocking her to sleep. Or just walking around with her in the baby carrier."

"You see?" Joe's arm curled around her waist in a gesture that seemed both natural and necessary. Hannah had to resist the urge to curl into his warmth. His chin rested briefly on her hair. Then drawing back, he concluded confidently, "Gus may like to think he's immune to all things that are sweet and hopeful these days, but I think just the opposite is true." A confident smile curved Joe's lips. "I think a new granddaughter is exactly what he needs in his life."

ISABELLA WAS IN BED BY eight-thirty, fast asleep. Gus followed soon after. Valerie returned from the grocery and went upstairs to read before turning in herself. Hannah sat in the center of the living-room floor, surrounded by baby gifts that hadn't yet been unboxed. Now here, she thought ironically to herself, was a situation when a husband would have come in handy.

As if on cue, Joe walked in. His hair was rumpled and dark-blond stubble rimmed the lower half of his face. He looked sexy and restless—as restless as she. He nodded at the mess around her. "Need any help?"

Mouth dry, Hannah watched the way the muscles rippled beneath his rumpled cotton shirt. "Sure."

He dropped down beside her, pants tightening around long, masculine legs and an exceptionally nice butt. He looked around, perplexed. "What is all this?"

At last, something to focus on beside the tantalizing green hue of his eyes. Ignoring the ache of loneliness deep inside her, Hannah embarked on a demonstration worthy of a TV game show hostess. "This is a stationary baby exerciser." She brought it close enough for him to see, setting it directly between them. "Isabella will be able to sit in the seat, and by using her feet, pivot all the way around to play with the various toys attached to the circular tray. She won't be able to actually go anywhere in it—which is what makes it safe—but shifting around to the different play stations will strengthen her legs."

Joe propped a forearm on an upraised knee. He had rolled the sleeves of his shirt up to just beneath his elbow. Crisp blond hair covered the suntanned hue of his skin. She found herself intrigued by the sinewy strength in his forearms, too.

She really had to get out more.

Had to start dating before she lost her mind...

Oblivious to the ardent nature of her thoughts, Joe asked, "Are you planning to use this contraption at the store?"

Hannah nodded, recalling what her daughter's pediatrician had said. "As much as I love carrying her around in the baby sling, she's not going to develop limb strength that way."

Joe helped her open another carton. "What's this?" he asked curiously as it came out in plastic-wrapped parts.

"A portable play crib." Hannah paused to consult the directions. Together, she and Joe folded it up and slid it into the compact carrying case. "I want to be able to take it down to the Mercantile, too. I can put it in the office during the day, along with the baby monitor, and she can nap there while I work on the books."

"Good idea." Joe took a mobile out of the box. "Where does this go?"

"On the play crib at work for now."

Joe turned the knob on it. The tinny sounds of "Twinkle, Twinkle, Little Star" filled the living room, making them both smile. "She's going to like that," he said.

As much as I like you? Hannah wondered, then pushed the thought away. He was leaving in a few days. She needed to remember that. Tensing, she stood. "I better get some of this stuff in my minivan, so it'll be ready to go to work in the morning."

Joe moved to assist.

Wanting to dispel some of the intimacy that had sprung up between them, Hannah said, "You don't have to help."

"I know." He was going to, anyway.

Sexual tension ricocheted between them. Swallowing, Hannah picked up the ExerSaucer and mobile. He followed with the portable play crib and stroller. Mindful of those already sleeping, they eased out the front door to the driveway.

The night sky overhead shimmered with stars and a brilliant yellow half-moon. Cicadas and crickets sang. A warm breeze rustled through the trees.

Hannah opened the tailgate. They worked in silence, turning items this way and that, fitting everything in. She shut the latch and turned. Her thigh bumped his knee. Suddenly, it was all so clear. She swallowed. "This…being just friends… isn't going to work. Is it?"

Joe shook his head. The next thing she knew he was stepping toward her, drawing her all the way into his arms. The hardness of his body pressed against the softness of hers, his embrace signifying the warm, sweet welcome of home. And Hannah knew, even before his lips touched hers—so tenderly and inevitably—that the time for holding back had passed. She might not want to be, but she was in love with Joe. Head over heels in love with him. And that, she thought as she put her arms around him and kissed him back with all the pent-up hunger of the past few days, was not going to change. Completely caught up in the moment, Hannah caressed the warm, solid muscles of his back. She loved the strong, hard, masculine feel of him. Never before had she been so tempted to let go of caution and take each moment as it came. All she knew was that the sensation of him pressed against her was wildly sensual. They were practically combusting, and all they had done was kiss.

Joe hadn't meant for this to happen. Hadn't meant to draw her close and kiss her again. He hadn't meant to get involved, with Hannah or her baby, hadn't meant to succumb to the demands of Hannah's irritable father. And he certainly hadn't intended that his cousin would be living here—albeit temporarily—with them, too.

But it had happened. He had become involved. To the point he was beginning to not want to leave.

Even though he knew he had to move on. He'd signed a contract. He was due to leave for Australia at the end of September. He was leaving Summit after Labor Day to finish his research on Big Bend National Park.

Hannah's life was here.

His was not.

So what the hell were they doing? And why, even now, couldn't he stop exploring her soft, sweet mouth and the silky give and play of her lips against his? Especially when he knew she wasn't into one-night stands any more than he was. Reluctantly, Joe stopped kissing her and stepped back. Hannah was trembling. He had felt—and now could see—the imprint of her nipples against the soft fabric of her blouse, just as he knew she could see the depth of his arousal. "Good thing we're not alone," she joked.

Joe's pulse raced. Lower still, desire roared. "We definitely need a chaperone." They paused to draw in jerky breaths.

"Joe…"

"I know." He held up a hand. "It can't happen."

Regret clouded her dark-brown eyes. "For all the reasons we've already been over."

"You're right."

"And yet?"

He lifted his hands in surrender. Breaking off the embrace without taking it any further had required a serious act of willpower. "I'm not going to lie about the way I feel," he whispered, gazing into her eyes. "I still want you." Hand cupping her nape, he brought her close and pressed a brief kiss to the top of her head. "I think I always will."

But wanting and doing were two different things and right now Joe had to do what was right—for all of them. And that meant walking away.

Chapter Eight

"Now that you're getting around better," Joe told Gus the next morning, after everyone else had left for work, "I'm thinking it might be time for me to move back to my cabin." Away from temptation. "At least at night."

Gus put down his newspaper. "Did you discuss this with my daughter?"

"Not yet. I wanted to get your take on the matter first."

"I think we need you here for a while longer. At least until you leave Summit. When is that again?"

"After Labor Day."

Gus mulled that over. "That gives me a little time. That is—" he regarded Joe steadily "—if you don't mind helping out."

"I don't mind," Joe said. He was glad to be there—to drive the old man around or help him up and down stairs, if Gus was feeling a little shaky.

"Good."

"I am curious, though." Joe carried his coffee into the room and settled in a wing chair, opposite Gus. "Initially, you didn't want any help recuperating. Never mind a non-family member like me underfoot all the time."

Gus shrugged, all sly innocence, and went back to his newspaper. "Might say I changed my mind."

Or motive, Joe thought, recalling the not-so-subtle matchmaking that had been going on.

"What happened between you and Hannah last night after I went to sleep?" Gus picked up his glass of apple cider.

Joe tensed. "What are you talking about?"

"Things were a little awkward this morning, between the two of you. What happened?" Gus persisted. "Did you move too fast?"

Joe wished that had been the only problem, almost as much as he yearned for the knack of assimilating seamlessly into a family. Joe reached for the sports page Gus had discarded. "I thought fathers were supposed to keep guys away from their daughters."

The older man exhaled, his regret obvious. "Exactly the problem. I think I did my job a little too well, while trying to weed out all the duds. Now she's pickier than I ever was, and with a baby, she needs a husband more than ever."

Joe wanted Isabella to have a father, too. But good parenting skills were not enough to propel anyone into marriage, least of all a woman like Hannah, who deserved only the very best. "I think that's for Hannah to decide."

"She wants to be married," Hannah's dad continued, amiably enough. "Just not to anyone I would choose, which is why you and I have to keep up the rancor between us."

"Forget subterfuge." Joe turned the page to a story on the Dallas Cowboys. "Hannah knows you like me."

Gus harrumphed. "I don't really like anyone."

Joe exhaled. "Let me put it another way. She knows you were trying to get the two of us together."

Gus's white brows furrowed. "You told her?"

Joe shrugged. "We don't have any secrets."

Gus looked impressed.

"You shouldn't read anything into that, either," Joe said.

Gus finished his cider. "I think I'd like a cup of coffee," he said.

Joe knew what had been in the pot was all gone. "I'll make some more right now." He stood.

"Not necessary," Gus said with a wily smile, standing, too. "We'll just head down to the Mercantile and get it there."

FOR A PERSON WHO COULD NEVER seem to fit into anyone else's family system, Joe thought, he was sure neck deep in all the drama of the Callahan clan. Unfortunately, not in a way Hannah was likely to appreciate. She was already ill at ease around him because of the sparks between them that were not going away. "You're supposed to be taking it easy," Joe reminded Gus.

"I'm not going there to work. We're just dropping by to say hello and have a cup of coffee on our way to..." Gus paused, contemplating a plausible excuse "...pick up some more apple cider."

Joe folded his arms in front of him. "There are two-gallon jugs of it in the fridge. Valerie brought them back last night." There was no way they could drink all of that today.

Gus feigned innocence. "I thought we were out."

"We're not."

Gus shrugged, unconcerned. "So we'll stop by the grocery store for something you need after we get coffee and chat a while at the Mercantile."

That would be fine, if Gus's motives were purely social. They weren't. "Hannah's going to know you're not there just to chat up the customers and hang out."

Gus shuffled toward the door. "So she'll see through me. So what? I want to see that coffee bar and whatever it is she's supposed to be reorganizing."

Joe shoved his hands through his hair. "I don't think any of that is finished yet."

"Good." Gus paused to make sure he had his wallet and keys. "Then there's plenty of time to keep her from messing up the Mercantile."

Joe strode ahead to get the door for him. "She is not going to appreciate this."

"I've got a thick skin. But—" Gus waved off the assistance with his good arm "—if you don't want to go, I can certainly drive myself…"

Hannah had warned Joe about this. "Your doctors all said no driving until after you've got the cast off and have finished physical therapy."

Gus frowned at the restriction. "My doctors worry too much."

Joe empathized with Gus's momentary lack of independence. However, it did not change his mind. "I'm driving you."

Gus considered arguing then gave up. "Fine."

Gus stared longingly at his vintage 1960s pickup truck, with the Mercantile logo still on the side, as he and Joe bypassed it for Joe's Land Rover. He didn't say a word as Joe drove them the short distance to Callahan Mercantile & Feed. "I may want to go over to the feed warehouse later, to check things out there," Gus said.

Great. That'll really thrill your daughter, Joe thought, getting out and sprinting around to assist Gus before the curmudgeon tried to do it all on his own.

Joe slid a hand beneath Gus's good arm, in an attempt to help him out of the SUV.

"I can manage on my own," Gus said stiffly.

Joe stayed close by, anyway, rushing ahead only long enough to hold open the door of the Mercantile. Even worse than the Closed For Reorganization sign on the front door, was what was going on inside.

"CLOSED UNTIL MONDAY!" Gus exploded, as Hannah had known he would. Which was why she hadn't told him.

Hannah glared at Joe as she glided through the stacks of shelving being moved to the front door. "Thanks a lot," she murmured to him under her breath, before turning back to Gus. "Dad. Please calm down."

He shuffled in, throwing up his uninjured arm. "How in tarnation can I possibly do that? You've been in charge here what—forty-eight hours—and you've already turned the place upside down!"

"I knew I was going to have to work fast to get everything I wanted accomplished," she defended herself.

Gus blinked. "There's more?"

As long as her dad was here, Hannah decided she might as well spell it all out and get it over with. "I'm starting a mail-order business. Hiring seamstresses to monogram items on demand—monogramming Western wear is big right now. I'm expanding all our outdoor items like camping and fishing gear. I'm going to carry tents and bedrolls, camp stoves and fuel. I plan to set up a center-store display to showcase the new items."

Two carpenters walked in. One carried a toolbox, the other precut sections of solid oak.

"I'm also putting in an old-fashioned counter with stools, serving premium coffees and teas for adults, ice-cream sodas and shakes for kids. Adding a cash register over at the feed warehouse, so our agricultural customers won't have to pay for their purchases here and then pick up there. They'll be able to do it all in one place. And last but not least, I'm cutting back on regular groceries that we currently sell—because we can't compete price wise on those items with the new chain grocery store—and expanding the selection of specialty foods like sourdough bread mix, fresh ground peppers, Texas barbecue sauces and the like."

"This will not be the same Callahan Mercantile & Feed."

"That's right. I'm taking it into the next century, Dad. At least for the next six weeks."

Gus stared at her a moment longer, then turned and stormed right back out the front door.

Hannah stared after him, her cheeks burning with a mixture of humiliation and disappointment.

Ruthann rushed up to Hannah. "I'll see he gets home and stay with him so he won't be alone." She looked at Joe. "You stay here and help Hannah. You move a lot faster than I do, anyway."

Joe assented with a nod.

Hannah avoided looking directly at him. "Valerie can show you what needs to be boxed up," she said.

"JUST OUT OF CURIOSITY, how long are you going to be mad at me?"

Hannah kept her glance away from Joe's handsome face and calmly continued taking down the stacks of canned items and dry goods that served as a window display. "How long you got?" She dropped the green wool blanket that had served as a backdrop into the box.

Joe braced a shoulder against the bay window frame and watched as Hannah peeled off a poster advertising a sale on beef jerky. "I figured my helpfulness today would buy me some reprieve."

He *had* worked relentlessly. Boxing up some items, unpacking, pricing and shelving others. That wasn't the point. "You figured wrong."

Joe pleaded his case with the persistence of a defense attorney. "I had no idea you were closed for business today."

Hannah simmered at the memory of her father storming in. "And if you had...?" she asked sweetly.

Joe stepped up into the now empty window with her. "I doubt I could have dissuaded Gus from coming down here. You know how he is once he gets his mind made up. Kind of like you."

Hannah doused the squeegee in the bucket of window cleaner. "Me!"

Joe took the wand from her and moved it back and forth where she could not reach without a ladder, along the very top of the glass. "You've been known to be cantankerous from time to time."

Content to let him take over for a moment, Hannah stepped back and peered at him through squinty eyes. "And about to get even more so," she warned without cracking a smile.

"That's okay." Joe dipped the squeegee back into the cleaner. "I'm strong enough to be able to handle a mood or two."

His words struck a chord. As much as Hannah hated to admit it, the string of recent events had left her very moody. She was deliriously happy one minute, completely stressed out the next. Hannah pressed her fingers to her forehead. "You're right," she said, after a moment. "It's completely unfair of me to blame my dad's reaction to everything I'm trying to accomplish here on you."

Joe did a third strip of window. "I gather the retooling was supposed to be a surprise?"

Her hands in her apron pockets, Hannah watched the ripple of muscles across Joe's broad shoulders, arms and back.

Her mouth went dry at the thought of what that spectacular body would feel like wrapped around hers. She pushed the unexpectedly erotic notion aside and said, "I had intended to get everything all set up and bring my father down here Monday morning before we opened for business, to show him then. I figured if everything was good to go he would be a lot less likely to be upset about all the changes I'm making."

"Instead—" Joe handed over the squeegee, at her wordless insistence "—Valerie tipped him off last night and he gets curious and walks in on the transition mess…"

"And blows a gasket." Hannah concentrated on cleaning the lower half of the big bay display window.

Joe stepped out of her path. "I talked to Ruthann a while ago. The good news is she is going to stay and make him dinner and keep him and Valerie company this evening."

Hannah tensed. "And the bad news?"

Joe caught her glance. "Your dad is still as riled up as a cougar with a thorn in his paw. Ruthann suggested I might want to take you and Isabella out to dinner."

Hannah batted her lashes at him in parody. "That's kind of you."

"Says the lady as she prepares to turn me down," Joe guessed. He stepped out of the display window and gave her a hand down, too.

"But I'm not up for any more questions on the new and improved Callahan Mercantile & Feed than I've already fielded today."

Joe picked up the bucket and walked out to do the outside of the glass. "The downside of living in a small town."

Hannah followed him out onto the sidewalk, enjoying the blast of fresh mountain air. "Explosions like Gus's make the rounds faster than you can hit speed dial on a phone.

Everyone's heard about it by now." Hannah lifted a hand in greeting at a customer driving by. "They're all going to want to ask for my version of events. Offer moral support. Or scold me. Depending on which side they're on."

Joe continued cleaning the window with steady even strokes. "People take sides on things like this?"

Hannah waved and nodded at yet another motorist who also happened to be one of their neighbors. "Oh, yes. It's as much a sport as rodeo around here."

Joe flashed a comforting smile. Finished, he followed her back in the door of the Mercantile. "You'll be proven right when you get everything up and running."

Hannah hoped so. Unfortunately, the events of the day, along with the turmoil the store was currently in, had left her feeling extremely discouraged. What if she had taken on more than she could handle? What if the rest of the town and their longtime customers reacted the way Gus had? This store was a fixture in Summit. Not only a place where tourists shopped. Was Gus right? Was she about to ruin a century and a half of success for the Callahan family? Take a business that had been in the black—if only barely, recently—and put it squarely in the red?

Joe placed both of his hands on her shoulders. "Call it a day and come back to my cabin with me," he said.

"And why would I do that?" Hannah retorted, her heart already racing with just the notion of saying yes.

Confidence radiated in his expression. He wrapped an arm about her shoulders, and led her toward Isabella's playpen at the rear of the store. The baby was just waking after a long and restful afternoon nap. Joe smiled down at Isabella and she smiled right back.

"You two deserve a break, and I am just the man to give it to you."

THIS WASN'T A DATE, JOE WARNED himself, as he put a skirt steak in marinade and then joined Hannah and Isabella in the dining nook that overlooked the deck.

Hannah sat Isabella on her lap, turning her toward the window overlooking the spectacular view of distant granite mountain and desolate plain.

Isabella was more intrigued by what Hannah was doing, however. She watched intently as Hannah dished warmed baby food from the jar, onto a child-size plate. "Look what Mommy has for you, Isabella. Yummy! Green beans." Hannah lifted the spoon to Isabella's mouth.

Isabella accepted the green puree, frowned at the unfamiliar taste, and pushed it right back out with her tongue. Green goop rolled down her chin and dripped onto the front of her pretty pink cotton dress.

Hannah made a face. "Would you check the diaper bag and see if there is a bib in there?"

Joe looked. "Nope."

Hannah sighed.

"Let's try this." Joe ripped off a square of paper towel and brought it over.

With his help, Hannah tucked it inside the collar of Isabella's dress. She attempted another spoonful of green beans. Wanting none of that, Isabella put up her hand and waved it away.

"Well, let's give sweet potatoes a try then," Hannah said cheerfully. "Those are supposed to be popular."

She offered a spoonful. Again, Isabella put up her hands to stop the food from making contact with her mouth. Hannah waited patiently until the way was clear and slipped a bite between Isabella's lips.

Once more, the sweet potatoes rolled right back out. This time, instead of simply letting the unwanted veggie drip down onto the paper towel, Isabella used both her hands to wipe the residue off her chin and onto Hannah's shirt.

Aware this was another first, Joe grinned. "Maybe we should try pears or peaches?"

Hannah shook her head. "The books say if she eats fruit first, she'll never eat veggies, so get her used to vegetables first." Hannah squinted at Joe, momentarily stymied, but not giving up. "I don't suppose you'd pretend to eat some of this?"

"No problem." Joe pulled up a chair and sat knee to knee with them. "Yum. Green beans," he said eagerly.

Hannah pretended to feed Joe some.

Isabella looked unimpressed.

Hannah tried to give Isabella some. Keeping her eyes firmly on Joe, Isabella pushed the spoon away with both hands.

"I think you're really going to have to actually eat it, to convince her," Hannah said, sending the spoon back his way.

Unfortunately, Joe thought so, too. He leaned forward. Isabella still cozily ensconced on her lap, Hannah slid the green beans between Joe's lips. The taste was…not great. The smile Joe plastered on his lips indicated otherwise. "Mmm. Wow. That is so delicious." He mugged enthusiastically, really hamming it up. "Mommy, I think you've got to try some of this, too!" He took the baby spoon from Hannah and gave her a bite.

"Mmm!" Hannah playacted as boldly as Joe had. "That is delicious. Isabella, would you like some?"

Giggling, Isabella pushed the food firmly away.

Joe picked up the spoon that had been in the sweet potatoes and coaxed her in Mandarin Chinese.

Entranced, Isabella watched as Joe brought the spoon closer.

Joe kept soothing. Isabella tasted the sweet potatoes and only pushed half of them out with her tongue.

Joe gave her another spoonful, while she relaxed on Hannah's lap, her head nestled between her mother's breasts. Then another...and another.

With every bite of sweet potatoes that went in, at least half came back out—and a quarter of that got smeared between Isabella's fingers and painted across her knees, arms and legs.

By the time they had finished, green beans and sweet potatoes were everywhere. But they had successfully gotten Isabella to eat her very first veggies, nevertheless.

Joe grinned. "High-five, Mom!" he said.

"High-five, D—," Hannah started to say, then blushed and turned away.

"THANKS FOR TAKING ONE for the team," Hannah told Joe an hour later, after Isabella had been bathed, dressed, and given a bottle of formula.

Joe had been tactful enough to pretend not to notice she had almost referred to him as Daddy. That didn't mean she had forgotten! She couldn't believe what she had almost said. She knew better than anyone that Joe was not her baby's father, even though she wished, on so many levels, that he was. He was so good with her little girl. So loving and kind and tender. And so good with her, too. Too good, Hannah thought, aware it would take very little to inspire her to fall even more in love with him.

Joe watched Hannah lay her sleeping daughter into the playpen in the living room and cover her with a blanket.

He moved closer. "I was happy to be part of such a big step for her."

Hannah had been happy to have him there, too. To the point she couldn't help but wish he would always be there for the two of them. Aware, however, that was not going to be the case, she reined in her emotions. "I couldn't have done it without you."

He shrugged off her praise with an easygoing smile. "Sure you could have. Although—" he grasped the sleeve of her blouse between his fingers "—your clothing probably wishes otherwise."

Hannah looked down in the direction of his gaze. "Ugh." Afraid the orange and green stains would set irrevocably if she didn't do something soon, Hannah hedged, "I don't suppose you have a shirt I could borrow...?"

"In my closet. You're welcome to wear any of 'em."

"Thanks." Trying not to think how it would feel to be enveloped in his clothing, Hannah went into the bedroom. She selected a blue-and-white pin-striped shirt that had been worn so many times the edges of the collar and sleeve were beginning to fray. It was big, soft and smelled like fresh air and sunshine. She slipped it on and put her own blouse in cool water to soak. She was still rolling up the sleeves on it when she walked back out to join him.

Joe was already on the deck, tending the grill. Suppressing the urge to embrace him and initiate a kiss, Hannah concentrated on being helpful. "What can I do?"

"What do you know about making guacamole and salsa?"

"A lot, as it happens." Glad to have something to occupy herself, Hannah gathered the necessary ingredients from the kitchen, brought them all outside and set up a work space on the picnic table. They talked about their favorite places in the Trans-Pecos. By the time the sun set over the mountains, dinner was ready. They wrapped spicy strips of steak in soft, warm flour tortillas, layered on the salsa and guacamole, and washed it all down with ice-cold bottles of Texas beer.

Hannah kicked back when they had finished. "That was heaven."

"We make a good team, in and out of the kitchen," Joe agreed with a wink.

Too good, maybe, Hannah thought, wishing he didn't look quite so handsome in the candlelight, wishing she didn't have quite so strong an urge to hold him close. Not just for now, but forever...

The night breeze blew across the deck. Unable to suppress a shiver, she wrapped her arms around her.

Noticing, Joe said, "I'll get you a jacket."

Not trusting herself to speak without giving her heart away, Hannah nodded.

He returned to fit it over her shoulders and stood there, looking down at her.

And suddenly she knew. Joe understood what she was feeling, because he felt the same. She could see the yearning in his eyes, feel it in his touch. Her mouth went dry, and she could feel the blood pounding in her veins.

Joe smiled. The ache inside her increased tenfold. He lifted a hand and rubbed his fingers through the ends of her hair. "You've got sweet potatoes here...and—" he grasped another strand, rubbing that between his fingers, too, "—green beans here..."

Hannah laughed it off. "That's what I get for having long hair."

"And," Joe added, wrapping one arm about her waist and slipping the other beneath her chin, "a baby."

He kissed her as if he meant it, with an insistence that

brought a rush of joy and a heady sense of release. Feelings poured through her, every bit as unstoppable as his embrace— a crazy jumble of lust, yearning, excitement and need. And Hannah knew, as she savored the touch and taste and smell of him, that more than anything she did not want this to end. Not any of it. Not their time together, not their friendship…not this evening.

Slipping her arms around his neck, she went up on tiptoe and threaded both her hands through his hair. She arched against him, pressing her breasts against his chest, her lower body against his thighs. She felt his arousal, hard and sure, as sure as his kiss, and then both his arms were wrapped around her. He was letting go all pretense of restraint, dancing her backward toward the door to the cabin, kissing her all the while.

They kept kissing, as they made their way to his bedroom. Until they bumped up against the side of his bed.

And still, Hannah did not want to stop. Did not want to give up on him, or the possibility that somehow, someway, everything might still work out. That they wouldn't have to say goodbye in a matter of days.

And why should they? she wondered fiercely, running her hands up and down his back. She had waited a lifetime for a man like Joe—a lifetime to feel so womanly, so desirable…so *alive*.

Still kissing him, she managed to toe off her boots. And then they were falling onto the bed, still holding each other. Bit by bit, thrill by thrill, they slowly undressed one another. Finally, they were both naked and throbbing and far too swept up in the moment to even consider walking away.

"First things first." Joe fumbled in the nightstand. The box was new. They laughed as he struggled with the plastic cover. And stopped chuckling when together, they finally managed to extract a packet. Joe's fingers shook as he opened the condom. Hers trembled when she helped put it on. And then he was lowering her back against the pillows, kissing her again, hot, breath-stealing kisses that melted her from the inside out.

Hannah kissed him back, again and again, their hands caressing each other's bodies, until there was no more holding back, only the need to be together as one.

"Now?" Joe whispered as she shuddered.

"Now," Hannah murmured, her heart slamming against her ribs. *Because I can't wait. Because, heaven help me, I've done what I swore I wouldn't, I've fallen in love with you, heart and soul….*

Joe lifted her against him and buried himself deep inside her. As their bodies merged, Hannah was certain she had indeed found pleasure at its highest level, and then there was nothing but the tidal wave of heat and need, lust and yearning, tenderness and compassion. Nothing but the taste of his lips and the feel of his hands…and the bliss of his body driving hers.

They soared again and again, until even that was not enough and together, they catapulted into a sweet, hot oblivion unlike anything Hannah had ever known.

Chapter Nine

"Look, it was bound to happen eventually, given everything we've experienced together," Hannah excused their behavior half an hour later, as they sat on opposite sides of the grill, toasting marshmallows over the fire. "It's no big deal."

Finally giving in to temptation and making love had felt like a big deal to Joe. A very big deal. He suspected it had meant more to Hannah than she was willing to admit to herself. But given the way she was looking at him, as if she wanted to trust him but wasn't quite ready, he did not challenge the illusion that it had been an impulsive, one time thing.

"We have weathered a lot the past month," Joe drawled, wishing he hadn't let her lead them back into their clothing and out of his bed quite so quickly. Maybe if they were still naked, he might have been able to convince her that they were not finished exploring their relationship. Of course if they'd still been naked, they wouldn't be talking now...

"The traveling alone took days." Hannah turned her marshmallow this way and that, making sure every side was equally golden brown and puffy. "And then there was the thrill of the adoption."

Joe smiled, recollecting the first time they'd laid eyes on

Isabella. "That was something, wasn't it?" he reminisced softly.

Hannah's eyes brimmed with happy tears as the sweet smell of caramelizing sugar filled the air. "It sure was." She took a moment, swallowed hard. "She is really going to miss you."

"And I'm going to miss her," Joe admitted thickly, recalling every precious moment, every up and down he'd had the privilege of experiencing with Isabella. Suddenly, he realized that Hannah wasn't so much protecting herself as she was protecting her child. As much as he wanted to, Joe could not blame her for that. Hell, in her place, he'd do the same.

"So now that we've gotten this—whatever it was—out of the way…" Hannah looked Joe square in the eye.

Joe knew what she wanted him to say. "We won't let it happen again."

She nodded, looking relieved. "Because our lives are far too complicated as it is."

"I NEED YOUR HELP," GUS TOLD Joe the following morning. Gus nodded at the pages of handwritten notes Joe had spread out on the kitchen table, next to his laptop. "You can get back to that later, can't you?"

Aware he was grouchy as hell this morning—which was what he got for being a gentleman instead of going after exactly what he wanted—Joe frowned and put on his game face. "What did you need?" he asked politely.

"Assistance in the attic. And we have to do it now. It will be too hot up there later in the day."

Joe followed Gus up to the third floor of the house Hannah had grown up in. It was a big, old-fashioned attic that ran the entire length of the big house. It was stuffed to the rafters with boxes, old furniture and every random thing imaginable.

"You could have a heck of a yard sale with this stuff," Joe said, examining a tarnished silver platter and the green glass vase that sat on top of it.

"If we ever got around to it," Gus agreed. "Hannah and I haven't been up here since her mother died. It was the kind of thing the two of them liked to do together."

Joe had seen photos of Hannah's mom around the house and heard a lot of stories about her from the locals. Izzie Callahan had been a beautiful woman who radiated gentleness and intelligence. Her presence was sorely missed. Although everyone agreed Hannah was a lot like her mom, in looks and temperament.

Gus picked up a ladder-back chair and set it next to a steamer trunk. "How is the pursuit of my daughter going?"

That depends on when you ask, Joe thought, pulling up a chair, too. Prior to their lovemaking the night before, he'd hoped he and Hannah were on the road to discovering something…lasting…if unconventional. Seeing the cool but purposeful way she had treated him this morning before she'd left for work, told him she had meant what she'd said the night before. And the hell of it was, she was right. The deeper they got involved with each other, the more it would hurt when they said goodbye. And they were saying goodbye in a matter of days now….

Aware Labor Day would be there before they knew it, Joe told Gus, "I'm not chasing her."

Gus gave Joe the kind of look that said he knew better. "She's not going to be easy to catch, you know."

That was certainly true. Hannah wasn't the kind of woman inclined to settle for less than what she wanted. And when it came to her life, and the man who might be in it, she knew exactly what she wanted. And it wasn't a frequent traveler like him. "I'm sure when the right man comes along, he'll know exactly what to say to get Hannah to say yes to his marriage proposal."

Gus took a moment to reflect on that. He rubbed a hand beneath his clean-shaven jaw. "As long as we're on the subject, anyone else around here you could possibly see her with?"

"Why are you asking me?" *Except to make me jealous as hell.* A plot, Joe was disinclined to admit, that was working.

Gus shrugged. "I'm an old man. What do I know about who would be right for her—if not you." He unlatched the trunk.

"It's not me," Joe said firmly, peeling back the lid. Hannah wanted someone who would help mend the tension between her and her father, not someone like him who disrupted whatever family he was around.

Gus began sifting through old newspapers and mailers. "Then there must be someone you've met around here I could set her up with to whom she would be receptive. What about Thad Garner, over at the E.R.? He's not bad looking. Single, professional, educated—like Hannah."

Jealousy twisted Joe's gut into knots. He was single, educated, and professional, too. "I've seen them talk—the night you were admitted to the hospital. I didn't notice any sparks."

Gus pointed to a stack of old black-and-white photos he could not reach. "What about Mason Enright? He's going to inherit his family's car dealership one day, and he sold her the minivan she's driving."

Joe snagged the pictures and handed them over. "I've never seen Hannah and Mason Enright together." Nor did Joe want to.

"Ever thought of putting down roots?" Gus asked, casual as ever.

Joe knew where this was headed. The back of his neck tensed. He wished Gus would quit his matchmaking. "That's never been my thing," Joe said evenly.

Gus handed another stack of pages to Joe. Reached in to get more. "Set in your ways already, hmm?" he chided.

Joe's hackles rose. "I'm not set in my ways."

"Then what would you call it?"

"Being smart."

Gus rummaged through more papers. "Ah. Here's what I've been looking for!"

It was a stack of old advertising notices. In terms of memorabilia, it was a treasure trove. "Has Hannah seen any of this?" Joe asked, glad to have the attention diverted from Hannah's love life.

"Probably not. Time she did, though. So let's get in that fancy SUV of yours and go down there."

HANNAH WAS STANDING NEXT TO Muriel Markham, the bookkeeper she'd hired to computerize and maintain their records, when the door to the Mercantile opened. Joe and her dad walked in. Joe was carrying a big cardboard box. Her dad looked askance at the construction going on. "Hannah, we need to talk," Gus ordered, as if he were still the one in charge. "Let's go to the office."

Doing her best to hide her aggravation, Hannah shook her head and did her best to maintain an attitude that honored her father but did not let him steal her newfound authority. "Isabella is napping in there, Dad," she said pleasantly.

"Storeroom it is, then." Gus insisted.

Joe set the box down on an unpacking table. He inclined his head toward the sales floor. "I'll wait out there."

"Stay with us," Gus ordered, leading the way.

Once they were in the storeroom. Gus didn't waste any time getting to the point. "The Mercantile is about tradition.

You're messing with that, Hannah. And I'll show you!" He handed over advertising for Callahan Mercantile & Feed, dating back decades. The copy in the ads and the overall design was beyond bad. Hannah shook her head, knowing nostalgia could only carry a business so far. "Dad, these ads may have worked on a local level twenty or thirty years ago, but I've looked at the tax returns for the last fifty years now."

Gus started to interject but she held up a hand.

She slipped back out to the table where the bookkeeper was set up, picked up a spreadsheet and returned to Joe and her dad. "And if you take inflation into account, we've lost one to two percent of income per year. If we want the Mercantile to survive long enough for Isabella and her children to inherit it, we have to put a new face on the business and expand into the mail-order arena, as well." She paused. "To be successful there, we have to add to our inventory and make improvements that customers are going to want."

They were also going to have to make a deal with a shipping company to deliver their goods, at discount, but Hannah figured that discussion could come later, when her dad had adjusted.

"You put in a newfangled cappuccino machine, you destroy the Old West ambiance. Joe agrees with me on this, don't you, Joe?"

Knowing he'd said no such thing, Joe protested. "Whoa now. This is between you and Hannah."

Hannah glared at Gus. "You gave me your word I could do as I wished as long as I was in charge! Are you going to honor that promise to me or continue interfering and undermining every little thing I do here?"

Gus looked taken aback by the iron in her tone—so much like the unyielding note in his.

A moment passed, then several more. The silence in the storeroom was deafening. Finally, Gus sighed. "You're right. What can I do to help?"

Looking frazzled but triumphant, Hannah turned to the wall of cardboard. "See what you can do about getting rid of the excess cases of campfire beans. Please."

GUS WENT TO THE FRONT PORCH to make the call. Emotions in turmoil, Hannah turned to Joe. "Et tu, Brutus?" she quipped.

"Hey." Joe angled a thumb at his chest. "I didn't want to bring him here. He insisted."

"You could have refused to drive him."

"He just would have called someone else to bring him down here."

Hannah sighed. "True." They walked over to the boxes containing the new cappuccino maker. "Do you agree with him that the high-end coffee is a bad idea?"

Joe shot her an aggrieved glance. "Didn't I just say I didn't want to be in the middle of this?"

"I know you have an opinion on the subject."

"I'm also smart enough to realize that taking any position will only cause more tension between the two of us."

Hannah waited for him to explain.

"You've barely spoken to me since we left the cabin last night."

Hannah reddened. "For heaven's sake!"

"Your father is ready to set you up with Thad Garner."

"He already tried. Neither Thad nor I are interested. Dad knows that. So if he mentioned it to you, he was testing the waters." She gave him a wary look. "What did you say?"

He shared her exasperation. "That I didn't see any sparks between you and Thad, either."

"You didn't admit…"

"That we…? No. Of course not."

Hannah breathed a sigh of relief.

"I don't kiss and tell."

The latent humor in his voice brought a smile to her face. "Well, just so you know, I don't, either."

"Then we're okay?" Joe asked.

"Of course." Their eyes met. "So back to the cappuccino maker…."

He groaned.

Hannah paced. "Maybe my dad has a point. This isn't the big city."

"True, but a lot of city folk come through here. They want more than twenty-five cent coffee in a paper cup. The markup on premium coffee being what it is, you'd be a fool not to take advantage of that demand."

Hannah circled closer. "I could still serve the tried-and-true for the locals."

"Like you said—for the business to survive, you have to take it into the new millennium…right along with everyone else."

"While still retaining all the Old West ambiance that has made us locally successful and drawn in the tourists." Hannah returned to the stack of Mercantile memorabilia and thumbed through it.

Gus came back in, triumphant. "I talked to the distributor for Cowboy Cuisine. One of their drivers is going to pick up the extra campfire beans this afternoon and credit our account. No charge to us."

Hannah gaped. "How did you manage that?"

"By promising Blake Kelleher, the sales rep, that you'd have dinner with him tomorrow night to discuss what else you might be ordering from their company."

"WHAT'S THE BIG DEAL?" Joe asked, when Gus had gone out to the sales floor to check on the doings there.

Hannah radiated unhappiness. "Blake Kelleher has had a crush on me for months now, and my dad knows that."

Joe tensed. "You're not interested in him?"

"I might have been if Blake had wanted kids, but he let me know the second time we went to dinner, back in March, that he doesn't like kids. So, I never went out with him again."

Joe disguised his relief. "How old is he?"

"My age. Thirty-one."

Next thing he knew, he'd be asking if the sales rep were cute, Joe thought, disgusted by his sudden pang of jealousy.

"I guess it won't hurt to go out with him for business reasons," Hannah conceded.

As long as business is all that is on the sales rep's mind, Joe thought.

Hannah walked out of the storeroom and paused in the office doorway to look in on Isabella. The infant was still curled up in the portable crib, sleeping, her teddy bear in her arms.

"I don't know how she can sleep through all that," Hannah mused over the racket the carpenters were making as they sanded down the new coffee and ice-cream soda bar. She kept going. Out on the sales floor, several people were gathered. Hannah quickened her steps and found Gus at the center of the commotion. Someone had gotten him a chair. He was pale and shaky. "What's going on?" she demanded.

"I overdid it a little," Gus snapped.

Ruthann hovered nearby. "I'm not surprised! It's too soon after your surgery for you to be out gallivanting around, Gus Callahan, and you know it!"

Hannah turned to Joe.

"I'll drive him home," he offered.

"And I'll go along to make sure he behaves himself this time," Ruthann promised.

And that quickly, they were out of there.

WORK WENT SMOOTHLY FOR the next few hours. Marcy and Valerie restocked shelves with new merchandise, while Hannah set up one window display of outdoor gear, another of traditional Mercantile inventory that included dry goods and blue jeans. She was nearly done when a fancy sports car stopped just short of Valerie's car, then backed up and pulled into a space close by. A cute guy with a trendy haircut and expensive clothing got out of the driver's seat. An elegant brunette in her early forties emerged from the passenger side. They headed for the Mercantile. Ignoring the Closed Till Monday sign on the front door, they walked on in.

Hannah climbed down from the window. "May I help you?"

"I'm Chris Elliott. This is Professor Leticia Hamilton. We're here to see Valerie Daugherty."

Valerie strode forward, a stony look on her pretty face. "You shouldn't have come."

Chris ignored her attempt to shoo them away. "People are starting to talk about why you left school the way you did," he complained.

Valerie folded her arms belligerently. "So?"

A muscle worked in Chris's jaw. "I expected you would put a lot more thought into it before you ended our relationship."

Valerie looked at the professor. "You're an expert in romance literature. What do you think I should have done?"

"I know that relationships and marriage are complicated affairs," Leticia Hamilton said carefully. "And that your parents are very distraught, as is the dean of the university.

None of us want to see you abandon your academic studies. As the head of the English literature department, I volunteered to talk to you and ask you to come back."

"I care about you, Valerie," Chris interrupted.

"We all do," Leticia Hamilton hastened to add.

"I'm not going back to the university," Valerie said flatly. She looked at Professor Hamilton, then Chris. "There's nothing you can do or say to convince me otherwise."

"If we could just talk privately," he pleaded.

"I'm sure if the three of us just sat down together, something could be worked out that would allow the two of you to coexist peaceably," Professor Hamilton urged.

"We already said everything that needs to be said," Valerie informed them. "I have to get back to work." She walked off.

Chris and the professor left reluctantly.

Hannah found Valerie. "Are you okay?"

Valerie nodded. "It's my fault, anyway. I should have known better than to get involved with a budding politician, when I saw what happened to Joe."

Hannah blinked. "What are you talking about?"

"His near-engagement to Selena Stanton, of course."

AFTER DINNER, HANNAH AND JOE took Isabella to the park. "Anything else happen at the store this afternoon?" Joe pushed the stroller over to the baby swings. "You and Valerie have both been awfully quiet since you got home."

Hannah briefly filled Joe in on the visit from Chris Elliott and Professor Hamilton.

Joe paused. "That's odd, don't you think? The two of them stopping by together?"

She nodded. "But that wasn't the only interesting thing that came up today." Joe held the swing steady while Hannah put Isabella in the seat.

"Valerie said you were once nearly engaged to Selena Stanton, daughter of the United States senator from Connecticut Stanton?"

"Obviously, this news upsets you for some reason," he remarked dryly.

She gave the swing a slight push. "It just makes me feel like I did in high school."

Joe exchanged little smiles with Isabella, before turning back to Hannah in frustration. "I don't follow."

"The boy I had a crush on told me he wasn't going to prom. Two weeks later, he turned around and asked someone else to go." She recalled the humiliation. "He thought he was doing me a favor, but I would have preferred he just be honest with me and tell me he didn't see us that way, than tell me something lame."

"Like…I'm not the marrying kind?" Joe interrupted, obviously able to see where this was going.

Hannah worked to keep her voice low. "That's the point." She smiled at Isabella before turning back to Joe. "Obviously, you *are* interested in marriage!"

"No," Joe countered patiently. He walked around behind the swing, so he could push Isabella. "I'm not. And it was my relationship with Selena that made me realize that."

Hannah leaned against the metal pole. "Now I don't follow."

"The Stantons are a close-knit clan. Everyone is expected to do a certain amount of schmoozing to raise campaign funds and secure victory for the senator. I gave it my all." Hurt and disappointment rang in Joe's tone. "My all wasn't good enough. The good senator suggested his daughter might be happier with someone more accustomed to the political life and better able to fit in with the Stanton family. And rather than take her father on, Selena gently showed me the door."

Hannah threw up her arms in frustration. "So she was not wife material herself. Why should that discourage you from ever marrying?"

"Because the same thing happened with my aunt Camille and uncle Karl and their two sons," Joe countered. "They were my closest relations, yet of their family, Valerie was the only one who really wanted me there. It was the same way with my own parents. They preferred doing things without me and I was their only son. And there were other instances, too. I used to get invitations to go home with friends, to see their families on spring or fall break, and it was always awkward."

Hannah edged closer, pausing to ruffle her daughter's hair. "It would be if you're with a family you don't know. It doesn't mean there is anything wrong with you."

He shrugged in resignation. "Some people are naturally family oriented. Others aren't. For whatever reason, I'm more of a loner than a joiner."

"You've fit in well with me and Isabella and my dad," she reminded him. So nicely, in fact, she didn't know what she was going to do without him.

"So far," he admitted cautiously.

She took over pushing the swing. "Ruthann and Valerie adore being around you, too."

"Again, easy to do, since both of them know they're not going to have to put up with me for long."

Reminded of how quickly time was passing, Hannah tensed. "You're still leaving Labor Day."

"Probably the morning after."

She didn't know why she had expected this would change. Just because they had made love the night before didn't mean Joe had any intention of sticking around any longer than originally planned.

Mistaking the reason behind her continued unhappiness, he cupped her shoulders and asked, "Why does it bother you so much to find out I was once nearly engaged?"

Hannah ignored the stab to her heart. "It doesn't."

He lifted a brow. Waited.

She drew a bolstering breath, realizing he wasn't about to let it go without an explanation of some sort. "It just makes me wonder if Senator Stanton's daughter has something I don't." Something that would make Joe want more than a momentary fling with her.

Eyes sparkling playfully, he drawled, "Well, as it happens, you do have something no other woman in my life has ever had."

Hannah batted her lashes, mocking his facetious manner. "And what's that?"

The next thing she knew, she was in Joe's arms once again. His lips fit against hers in a tender, gentle kiss. "My heart," he said.

Chapter Ten

"Sorry," Joe said from the doorway of the kitchen. Just after midnight, his voice was a sexy rumble in the late-night stillness of the house. "I didn't know anyone was still up."

Hannah hadn't known he was awake, either. He'd retired to his room hours ago.

Still glowing from the confession he had made and still confused about the fact she could be so enamored of someone who was only going to leave her in the end, she smiled and sat back wearily in her chair. "It's okay. You can come in."

She took in his dark-gray jersey sleep pants and white T-shirt. In turn, he scanned her bright-pink capri pants, pale-pink tank top, matching sleep-cardigan and fuzzy slippers. "I was just about to raid the refrigerator," Hannah murmured. "I presume you're here for the same reason?"

"Caught me red-handed." He ambled closer. "What do we have?"

"Cold fried chicken, sourdough biscuits and Texas peaches. And milk to wash it down."

Joe held the refrigerator door, while Hannah juggled serving dishes. She carried it all to the table. He brought the jug of milk, and followed that up with plates, silverware and napkins.

Hannah went back to the fridge for the butter dish. "What's keeping you up so late?" she asked over her shoulder.

"I was working on my book."

They sat opposite each other. "I haven't forgotten about proofreading for you. I plan to do that tomorrow evening, if that's okay with you."

"It's fine. Although given all you've got on your agenda…"

She came up out of her chair, and put a finger to his lips. "A promise is a promise. I'm just sorry it's taking me so long to get to it."

"I'll be here a few more days, before I head to Marfa for Labor Day weekend."

She realized with a pang that she had less time left with Joe than she'd thought. "You're attending the Lights Festival?" It made sense for him to go and see it in person if he was going to write about it. The mysterious phenomenon was a big draw for tourists in the area.

He nodded. "I want to include it in my book."

She had known this day was coming. Still, the knowledge that soon Joe would no longer be a part of her daily life was hard to deal with. She forced herself to smile cheerfully. "When are you leaving Summit?"

"I have to be in Big Bend, for a private tour with a national parks' representative, the Wednesday after Labor Day, so I'll probably leave Summit on Tuesday."

"It's tradition for the Mercantile to host a cookout for store employees and their family and friends on Labor Day. We usually have it here. If you're still in town and would like to attend, you are of course invited."

Joe nodded. "Sounds good."

Hannah tried not to think about the fact that might be the last time she would see him, at least for a very long time.

He cut into a peach. "So what's been keeping you up?"

Glad to talk about something else, she sighed. "I was going through some of the memorabilia you and Dad brought down to the Mercantile. It's pretty interesting. I especially liked those black-and-white photographs from years past. Anyway, it got me thinking. Maybe Dad's right about not polluting the Old West aura of the store with modern day cappuccino machines."

"You've already built the coffee bar. The finish on it is drying as we speak."

"That's going to be okay—the way it's designed is in keeping with the theme of the Old West, and the distressed finish is reminiscent of an old saloon. But I'm thinking we should build another cabinet to hide all the high-tech equipment from view behind the bar, and put up a long black chalkboard on the wall, where the beverages could be listed. For instance, we could call the steamed milk and cinnamon concoction *Cowboy Coffee*. Espresso could be called *Revved Up Round Up Coffee*—for that extra punch. And an iced latte would be a *High Country Cooler*."

"Wow. You've really put a lot of thought into this," he said, clearly impressed.

Her eyes lit up from his praise. "Wait…there's more. We could sell insulated souvenir mugs that look like tin, leather or granite on the outside. Our regular take-out cups could be decorated with the old black-and-white photographs and the Mercantile insignia and new Web site address."

"Synergy."

"Hey." Hannah kicked back in her chair, her knee accidentally bumping up against his in the process. "If it worked for Martha Stewart building her empire, it could work for me."

He left his leg where it was. The heat of his body warmed hers. "How long will it take you to implement all this?"

Realizing she was already way too aware of Joe, Hannah

shifted her knee backward, so they were no longer touching. "The Web site will be up within a few weeks—in plenty of time for the holiday rush on ornaments and gifts. I imagine the disposable travel cups will take about the same amount of time, once I contract with a printer. The souvenir mugs a lot longer. But it's all doable."

Joe stood and carried his empty plate to the sink. "Gus is going to be so proud of you."

She followed suit. "I wish."

"He is." Joe looked deep in Hannah's eyes. "And he will continue to be. He just has a hard time showing it."

Her throat thickened with emotion. "Your support has meant a lot to me."

He wrapped his arms around her and pressed his lower half to hers. "You're easy to support."

A wave of yearning sent warmth flowing through her. Her response was all it took. Joe flattened a hand against her spine, bringing her closer still. Then his lips were on hers again, tempting, hot, persistant. Her lips softened under his, then parted to allow him more intimate access. Over and over he kissed her, until the room faded away and all that mattered was the feel of their bodies pressed up against each other. Hardness to her softness. Male to female. And a need that would never go away.

Hannah sighed her pleasure. Even as she forced herself to be sensible again. She shifted her hands from his shoulders to his pecs. "Joe…"

"I know." Joe drew back. Resignation mixed with the ardor in his green eyes. He dropped his hold on her respectfully and moved away. "It's not going to happen—we're not going to make love again."

HANNAH KNEW SHE HAD DONE the right thing, walking away from any further physical intimacy with Joe. But that did not chase away the ache of loneliness that only he could assuage. She was still contemplating the loss when Gus appeared in the doorway of the kitchen the next morning. "I'm ready to go to work any time you are," he announced heartily.

"Actually, Dad." She paused to feed Isabella another spoonful of rice cereal and mashed banana, before turning back to her father. "I think you might want to work here today."

Gus pulled up the chair next to Isabella and carefully lowered himself into it. "What could I possibly do here?" he demanded.

Hannah noted her father's color was good today. She wanted it to stay that way. "I want you to go through the old photographs and pick out a dozen or so for me to use on the take-out cups and in our new advertising campaign for the Web site. If you could get that done today, I could get them to the printer. In the meantime we could have paper sleeves made for the existing cups and use those until we get our own specialty ones made up."

He watched Hannah feed Isabella her last bite of mashed banana. "I can do that at the store."

Mindful of the need to get Isabella feeding herself finger foods, Hannah took the empty dish away and put a palmful of puffed corn cereal on her daughter's high-chair tray. "There's no place in the office for you to spread out the way you'd need to."

Isabella flirted with Gus, smiling shyly and batting the lashes of her dark almond-shaped eyes. Gus was hard-pressed not to smile. "Then I'll set up a card table in the storeroom," he said.

She pretended not to notice the eye contact between grandfather and granddaughter. She poured her dad a cup of coffee and a glass of apple cider. "The pick-up of the extra two hundred boxes of ranch-style beans is set for today, along with the delivery of the new items we're going to be stocking. It's going to be too chaotic."

"So in other words," Gus grumbled, watching as Isabella attempted to pick up a puffed-corn ball with her fingers, "you want me out of the way."

Hannah flushed. So much for telling her dad what she needed from him, and expecting it to do any good. She broke two eggs into a pan. "You overdid it yesterday, Dad."

He watched her scramble the yolks. "So I won't push so hard today," he argued back, as Joe walked in.

Hannah looked at Joe, hoping he would back her up on this. Instead, he lifted his hands in front of him and sidestepped the contretemps.

Thanks, heaps, she mouthed at him.

Hannah turned back to her dad. The corners of Gus's lips lifted slightly as Isabella palmed a corn puff and awkwardly tried—and failed—to maneuver it to her mouth. Feather-soft brows knit in concentration, she reached determinedly for another.

Hannah added salt and pepper to her dad's eggs and popped two pieces of whole wheat bread in the toaster. "Please, Dad, just do this for me. So I don't have to worry."

He started to argue, then stopped. "Fine." He chortled approvingly as Isabella finally managed to shove a corn puff into her mouth. Grinning his approval, he wordlessly added more dry cereal to her high-chair tray. "I'll work on the photos here."

Hannah sighed in relief, glad her father was finally beginning not to just accept Isabella's presence, but actually interact with her a bit. "Thank you," she said softly.

Gus shot her a cantankerous look. "Don't thank me yet. You haven't seen what I picked out."

DESPITE HIS QUERULOUS ATTITUDE, Gus spread out the photos on the dining-room table even before Hannah and Valerie left for work with Isabella in tow.

Glad he'd managed to stay out of the middle of the Callahan family argument, Joe set up his laptop and went to work in the kitchen.

At nine-thirty, Gus shuffled in, an impatient look on his face. "We're out of lightbulbs and the light in the half bath under the stairs is out."

Knowing Gus could not be expected to go up and down the stairs all morning every time he wanted to use the lavatory, Joe pushed away from his laptop computer. "I'll run to the hardware store and pick some up." He paused, able to see Gus was already as restless as a long-tailed cat around a rocking chair. "Want to ride along with me?"

Gus shook his head and looked insulted for having been asked.

Empathizing with Hannah's dad, knowing it must feel like he had a babysitter all the time these days, Joe headed out the door. He was gone twenty minutes. Which was all the time it took for Gus to disappear. Swearing, Joe went out to the detached garage. Gus's vintage pickup truck was no longer parked inside. It wasn't too hard to figure out where he had gone.

Joe drove back toward Main Street. He got there just in time to see Gus's pickup truck start to turn into one of the slanted parking spaces in front of the Mercantile, only to narrowly miss the tail end of a fancy sports car as it backed out of the adjacent space. That wasn't Gus's fault, Joe noted, tensing at the near miss. The driver hadn't looked before backing out. But the extra-wide angle Gus's truck took to avoid a collision *was* Gus's fault.

Too late, Gus tried to overcorrect his mistake. With one arm still in a cast and a sling, it wasn't easy.

Joe winced as Gus's pickup truck jumped the curb and plowed into a fire hydrant.

The simultaneous boom and sound of crunching metal were followed by a geyser of water, spilling onto the sidewalk.

Joe parked his SUV and hurried to check on Gus at the same time as Hannah and her entourage came running out of the store.

Gus held up his good hand, staving off a multitude of first aid. "I'm all right!"

Joe was relieved to see that he apparently was.

"Dad, for heaven's sake! What are you doing driving?" Hannah demanded.

With difficulty, and an assist from Joe, Gus got down from the cab. He was pale and shaky, but otherwise seemed all right.

"I thought I'd come down to the store and see how things were going," he groused, stepping to avoid the fountain of pouring water.

The baby in her arms, Hannah waded through the growing river on the sidewalk. She glared at Joe, like it was all his fault! "You let him drive?" she cried.

"Of course he didn't," Gus interrupted, even more grouchily. "Had to send him on a fool's errand before I could get anywhere near my own vehicle!"

"Fool is right," Joe muttered, sorry he had taken his eyes off the old man for one second.

"There's only one fool around here," Ruthann said, marching up to Gus. "Honestly," she said, hands on her hips, looking like she wanted to wring his neck, "some times you don't have a lick of sense, Gus Callahan!"

Hannah looked like she seconded that sentiment.

Valerie stepped forward. "Mr. Callahan? Maybe you'd like

to come inside and sit down for a second. Have something cold to drink."

"That's a good idea," Hannah said, still wading through the water, visibly distressed.

Hannah had Valerie and Ruthann take Isabella back inside the Mercantile, while she stayed outside to do damage control.

Twenty minutes later, order had been restored to the scene. The water supply to the damaged fire hydrant had been shut off by the fire department. A Summit County sheriff's deputy had written up an accident report, citing Gus for reckless driving.

Joe drove Gus's pickup to the local garage and left it there for repair while Hannah and Ruthann took Gus to his physician's office to be checked out.

"Your dad okay?" Joe asked Hannah when she returned to the store an hour later.

Hannah smiled at her daughter, who was strapped into the baby carrier on Joe's chest. Isabella was facing outward and enjoying the view from up high, while chewing on a teething ring she held clutched in one hand. She gurgled in pleasure when her mama tenderly kissed her cheek. And then she clutched a fistful of Hannah's hair and held tight.

Hannah winced at the pressure, and used both hands to extricate the little fingers from her hair. "Dad's fine. Ruthann took him home."

Isabella gurgled happily again and grabbed on to the collar of Hannah's blouse.

Thrown off balance, Hannah bumped into Joe's side. She placed a soft hand on his bicep, steadying herself.

Trying not to think how great it had felt to have those same hands undressing him, Joe kept the conversation on Gus's accident. "It could have happened to anyone."

Hannah leaned down and kissed her daughter's arm.

Isabella giggled again and stuck her fingers in Hannah's mouth.

Hannah responded with playful kissing sounds that made Isabella smile all the more. "It wouldn't have happened if he'd had the sense not to be driving," Hannah said, still smiling at Isabella.

Joe could see she was worried about her dad. "It's just the way he is, Hannah."

"Yeah, well, he's not going to be around much longer if he doesn't start using better judgment," she said. And then she burst into tears.

Joe steered her out of the store aisle and into the office. He shut the door behind them and wrapped an arm about her shoulder, wishing he could take her all the way into his arms.

Isabella leaned back against Joe's chest, studying her mother pensively.

"It's okay." Joe squeezed Hannah's shoulder again.

"It's not." She leaned forward to pluck a tissue from the box on the desk. "He's driving me crazy!"

Joe sat on the desk. He spread his legs and guided Hannah down to sit on one thigh, so she and Isabella were facing each other. He draped his arm around Hannah's shoulders and pressed a comforting kiss in her hair, the way she had just done to Isabella. "If you're going to be mad at your dad," Joe chided softly, "you may as well be angry with me, too. I'm the one who let him duck out on me."

Hannah blew her nose. "I shouldn't have asked you to try and contain him. My dad can't be reined in. I know that." She flashed a watery smile at her daughter. "He's my problem…my responsibility."

"Look." Joe waited until she met his gaze before he continued. "We're friends. You needed help and had every right to ask me. I'm the one who screwed up. I knew Gus was fit to be tied, stuck at home recuperating while big changes were going on at the store. I should have never left him alone this morning."

Hannah swallowed, listening.

Isabella dropped her chew toy and held on to Joe's shirt with one hand and Hannah's blouse with the other. "The point is," Joe soothed, "he did something foolish and embarrassed himself. No one got hurt. Life as we know it is going to go on. The question is…are you going to be okay?"

Hannah squared her shoulders resolutely. "Of course."

He studied the vulnerable look in her eyes, so at odds with the determined tilt of her pretty chin. Wanting more than ever to protect and help her, he asked, "How about I take Isabella back to the house with me and you just worry about work here today?"

Hannah raked her teeth across her lower lip. "You're sure?"

Joe nodded, wanting more than ever to do whatever he could for Hannah and her family. "After what happened this morning, I owe you one."

DETERMINED TO GET HOME to her baby girl as soon as possible, Hannah worked through lunch and finished up for the day at five-thirty. She drove the short distance home, grabbed the mail from the box and walked in the back door.

Ruthann was standing at the stove, making dinner.

Valerie, who'd left the store at the same time, came in behind Hannah.

"Where is everyone?" Hannah asked, warming at the homey family scene.

Ruthann smiled. "Joe went to the grocery for milk and eggs. Isabella is exercising on her play mat in the living room.

Your dad is reading one of his news magazines and watching over her until Joe gets back."

Hannah blinked, not sure she had heard right. "The dad who didn't want me to adopt her."

Ruthann stopped stirring the beef stew long enough to point a wooden spoon at her in lecturing fashion, just as Hannah's mother would have done. "You should go and talk to him. He feels terrible about what happened today." Ruthann caught Valerie by the shirtsleeve. "You. Stay and help me fix a salad and get some biscuits in the oven."

Valerie grinned. "Yes, ma'm."

Curious about what was going on, Hannah moved soundlessly through the shadow-splashed foyer to peer around the edge of the portal. She saw Isabella lying on her back on her quilted mat, her infant play gym of touch and learn toys in an arc above her. Hannah noted that Isabella could see Gus clearly from where she lay. She seemed to be—through the nonsensical cooing sounds she was making—trying to tell her grandpa about the animal figures she was touching and exploring.

Hannah's heart lightened as she noted Gus doing his best to participate, too.

"Yes, that's a lion, all right. And that's an elephant."

Isabella babbled all the more, and looked at Gus as if inviting him to come down and play with her. "Honey, I wish I could get down on the floor to play with you. But I can't."

With a smile on her face, Hannah remained out of sight, watching as Isabella kicked her arms and legs and looked at Gus all the more urgently.

"You're right." He chuckled. "Actually, I could get down there. The problem is I wouldn't be able to get back up. And then where would we be? Calling the fire department or EMS again? I don't think so."

Isabella batted one of her toys and smiled at him as it dangled on its loop.

"So we'll have to be content to look at each other," Gus continued, gentle as you please. "Hang out and get better acquainted this way...."

The doorbell rang, to Hannah's frustration, interrupting the blissful moment. On the front porch, more voices sounded. Male voices. Gus stopped talking abruptly, picked up his news magazine with his good hand and pretended to be lost in thought. Isabella continued cooing.

The door opened behind Hannah. Joe walked in, bag of groceries in hand.

He wasn't alone.

HANNAH, JOE NOTED WITH satisfaction, looked about as happy as he was that Blake Kelleher had arrived to take her to dinner.

"Oh my gosh," Hannah murmured, looking at Blake Kelleher, a becoming blush on her face.

"You forgot about our date, didn't you?" Blake Kelleher handed over the big bunch of flowers he had in his hand.

"Business meeting, and yes, I confess I did. But not to worry," she said graciously, recovering nicely. "I can be ready in five minutes. Just let me say hello to my daughter and then I'll run upstairs to change."

Gus levered himself out of the chair, moving toward them with a welcoming smile on his face. He shook hands with Blake and exchanged pleasantries. Hannah picked up Isabella and introduced her to Blake.

Blake reacted with as much enjoyment as a person who had no interest in having children could be expected to react. Hannah looked a little hurt, then disappeared up the stairs, Isabella in her arms.

Joe went into the kitchen to get a cold drink for their guest. Then he slipped out and went up the stairs himself. He rapped on Hannah's door.

She opened it a second later, Isabella still in her arms. "If you're here to tell me to hurry up..." she warned.

On the contrary, Joe did not want her to leave on this date at all, especially with a guy who did not seem to realize what a truly extraordinary little girl Hannah's daughter was. He shrugged and offered affably, "I figured I'd see if you needed a hand with Isabella while you did whatever you have to do."

Hannah buried her face in the fragrant softness of her daughter's smooth black hair, drinking in the baby-soft smell of her, then with a reluctant sigh and a wistful look, handed Isabella over to Joe. "Come on in. The truth is, I could use a hand."

She disappeared into the closet, then came out with a dress on a hanger and a pair of high heeled sandals in her other hand. A stop at the dresser had her pulling out another handful of frills and lace. With Joe staring lustfully after her, she disappeared into the adjacent bath, shutting the door behind her.

Joe heard the swish of clothing hitting the floor. The sound of water running. Cosmetics opened and shut. More moving around. The door opened once again.

"About that proofreading," Hannah said, looking incredibly beautiful in a wine-colored summer dress that hugged her slender figure and left most of her arms bare.

He grinned, knowing at this rate she'd never get around to doing him the favor she had promised. "It can wait."

She picked up a hairbrush and ran it through her hair. "I know you think I'm not going to do it." She set it down on the dresser and picked up a bottle of perfume.

"I think the intention is there." It was all he could do not to groan as she spritzed a little behind each ear, the nape of her neck, between her breasts.

"It will get done," Hannah reassured him.

The truth was he would much rather spend what time he had left in Summit with her. But not sure how that announcement would go over, he merely smiled. "I believe you."

"No, you don't. But that's okay." Hannah turned back to the mirror. She paused to apply a fresh coat of lipstick, then walked toward him and once again took Isabella in her arms. "I wish I didn't have to leave you," she whispered, looking first at her daughter and then longingly at Joe.

Joe wished that, too. He wished the three of them could spend this night and every one to come, together, just hanging out. But since that wasn't possible... "I'll see your dad has more time with Isabella," he promised.

Hannah's dark-brown eyes widened. "You knew he was talking to her?" she ascertained softly.

Joe was glad Hannah had observed it, too. "On and off, all afternoon, whenever he thought no one was around."

Contentment shone in Hannah's expression. "He's really going to love her one day, isn't he?"

Joe nodded. "I think he already does."

Chapter Eleven

"You're thinking the same thing I am, aren't you?" Joe whispered to Isabella. They swung back and forth on the chain-hung front-porch swing. "Where are they?"

It was after eleven. Hannah and Blake Kelleher had left for their business dinner hours ago.

There'd been no word since.

"We could call your mommy's cell phone, of course," he told the still wide-awake Isabella. He felt like the chaperone for Hannah. When what he wanted was to be the reason she needed a chaperone. "But I don't really think it's necessary. Yet. What is necessary is finding a way to put you to sleep, little darlin', 'cause it is way past your bedtime."

Isabella snuggled against his chest, her hands clutching his shirt. Aware it was a little chilly, he made sure the knit blanket was wrapped around her, the soft-pink cotton knit cap covering her head. "It would help, of course, if you would consent to take this bottle of formula I fixed for you," Joe said.

He offered the bottle.

Isabella looked directly into his eyes and pushed it away with one hand.

"You just don't want to go to sleep until your mommy comes home, do you?"

Isabella made a nonsensical reply and turned her head at the sound of a car making its way up the street. Seconds later it rolled to a stop at the curb in front of the Callahan residence.

Joe knew the polite thing to do would be to pick up Isabella and go in the house, so Hannah could say her good-night to Blake Kelleher in private. But something in him—something primitive and male—railed against it, so instead he sat where he was, with Hannah's baby snuggled in his arms, waiting for her to make her way up to the porch.

It didn't take long.

She said her goodbye to Blake on the sidewalk, not even waiting for him to drive away before she joined them on the porch. "What have we here?" she murmured.

Joe scooted over. Hannah sat down next to him on the swing. Her eyes on her daughter, she held out her arms. Isabella chortled happily. Joe made the transfer.

"What are you still doing awake, little pumpkin?" Hannah asked her daughter, smiling down at her in the soft glow of the porch light.

"She wouldn't go to sleep. Ruthann, Valerie and I all tried rocking her, to no avail. She was waiting until you got home."

He handed her the bottle. Isabella clutched the bottle with both hands, her eyes on Hannah's face. She sucked greedily, then stopped and smiled, milk bubbles appearing on her lips. Hannah smiled back. Isabella drank some more and closed her eyes.

Two minutes later, the bottle was empty and she was asleep.

Hannah lifted her upright and turned her so the baby's cheek was resting on her shoulder while she continued rocking gently in the swing. "I know I should put her in her bed," she sighed.

Joe knew exactly how Hannah felt. "But you can't put her down."

They exchanged commiserating smiles. "It was so hard being away from her this afternoon and evening. I felt so guilty for not being here."

Joe breathed in the light, feminine fragrance of Hannah's hair and skin. His body heated as she relaxed into the curve of his arm. "You shouldn't have—she did fine."

Hannah rested her head on his shoulder. They continued rocking. Joe savored the feeling of togetherness. "She's come a long way in just a couple of weeks," she whispered.

It was all he could do not to run his fingers through her hair. But touching her would likely lead to kissing her, and kissing her would lead to wanting to make love to her…and making love to her would lead to wanting to stay….

"Going from being comfortable with only you—" Joe said.

"And you," Hannah added.

"—to accepting Ruthann and Valerie, and even Gus."

Hannah subtly shifted away from him, so they were no longer touching from shoulder to thigh. She ran a hand up and down the baby's spine, caressing her gently. "That was so wonderful, to see him talking to her."

"It's only going to get better," Joe predicted. And the hell of it was, he would not be here to see it happen. He'd be off in Australia, half a world away, researching his next project….

Frustrated that the idea of escape was offering none of its usual allure, Joe frowned.

"So how was your business dinner?" he asked lightly. "Was Gus's wish granted?" Another unprecedented wave of jealousy twisted his gut. "Did it turn into something more?" Something that could lead to marriage…and the husband Gus Callahan wanted for his only daughter?

"Hardly," Hannah said dryly. "The business side of the evening was good, though. Well worth my while, in fact."

The pleasure in her low tone brought him contentment, too. "What happened?"

She shifted around slightly, to look at Joe. Excitement glimmered in her pretty eyes. "I got Blake to agree to cut our shipping costs by fifty percent if we order everything in bulk twice-monthly, instead of whenever we run out of something. That way he gets credit for large sales, it reduces their book-keeping and scheduling and it will make my life a lot easier, too, now that we have the computerized inventory system all set up. That's going to save us time and money and will increase the Mercantile profits right away."

"Gus is going to be so proud of you."

Hannah nodded hopefully. "Once he adapts to change. And speaking of my dad...and the others...where is everyone?"

"Gus went to bed around nine-thirty, shortly after Ruthann went home. Valerie went to sleep around ten-thirty." Which meant they were alone. The two of them could sit out here all night—talking—and no one would be the wiser.

Unfortunately, that wasn't Hannah's plan. Her lips took on a rueful twist as she stopped the swing and stood. "Speaking of bed, I guess I better put Isabella down."

"Let me give you a hand." Reluctantly, Joe eased off the swing and moved soundlessly toward the portal. He held the front door while Hannah eased inside and carried Isabella up the stairs. Aware she could take it from there, he stayed on the porch, fighting to get his feelings under control.

A minute later, Hannah walked back out on the porch. She picked up her handbag, which was right where she'd left it next to the swing. Gliding closer, she lifted her face up to his. "Aren't you coming in?"

"Not," Joe said gruffly, giving in to the passion that had been dogging him all evening, "before I do this." He took her in his arms.

He heard her soft gasp. Felt the melting of her body. And then his lips were on hers, and she was kissing him back, with no reservation. Joe sifted his hands through her hair and tilted her head slightly to allow him better access. Their kiss deepened all the more, and the breath caught in her chest. She went up on tiptoe, wrapping her arms about his neck and holding him close. Letting him know that this was no passing fling. The feelings they had were not going to fade.

Hannah had been thinking about Joe all evening. Wishing she could be right here with him, just like this. To find he wanted her just as much was like a wish come true. And though she had never been one to live in the moment, with no view to the future, she found herself wanting to do just that with Joe. Again and again, she kissed him, until at last they slowly drew apart once again.

Hannah looked into Joe's eyes and saw everything she had ever wanted there. "I missed you tonight," she whispered thickly.

Joe tightened his grip on her possessively. "I missed you, too."

JOE'S CONFESSION STAYED with Hannah the rest of the night. It was with her as they parted company in the foyer and she went upstairs and got ready for bed. It was with her as she climbed beneath the sheets, and tossed and turned, trying to go to sleep. It was with her in her dreams and on her mind when she woke up the next morning.

She'd never been the kind of woman to pursue a man.

There had been no need for that.

If a guy hadn't hit on her, she had assumed he was not interested in her and put the possibility of anything happening between them out of her mind.

With Joe, it was different.

Joe made her want to see if she could seduce a man.

Joe made her want to wage a campaign to make him fall for her as surely as she was falling for him.

Joe made her want to come up with a way that would entice him to forgo his adventuring ways and make a home right there in Summit, with her and Isabella.

And that was crazy, she decided, as she went in to wake her still-sleeping baby girl and carry her down to the kitchen for breakfast. She found everyone else already there. Joe was standing at the stove, pouring pancake batter onto a sizzling hot griddle. Valerie was making coffee. Gus was sitting at the table while Ruthann set a glass of milk in front of him.

It was a warm and cozy family scene, the kind that had been in short supply since her mother died. Even though three of the participants weren't technically family....

Wishing she'd taken the time to do more than brush her teeth and hair and throw a robe on over her pajamas, Hannah said, "You're all up early."

"Actually—" Joe left the stove long enough to help her get Isabella situated in her high chair "—you're up late."

Hannah glanced at her watch and blinked in surprise. It was an hour later than she usually got up.

"Wow. I must have been more tired than I realized."

"Not surprising, given how hard you've been working," Ruthann sympathized, setting the table for five adults.

Hannah mixed up a dish of rice cereal and mashed banana for Isabella. She sat down next to the high chair.

"Why don't you take the day off?" Valerie asked.

Valerie had no idea how good that sounded, Hannah

thought. "I can't. We haven't set up the coffee bar and ice-cream soda fountain yet."

"Can't do that until the freezer case is installed and the plumbing put in, and none of that is scheduled to be done until later this afternoon," Ruthann pointed out.

"So you may as well at least take the morning off," Gus said.

Hannah stopped feeding Isabella long enough to stare at her dad. "You are telling me not to go into work," she repeated, dumbfounded.

He managed a small shrug. "It would be different if the store were open, but—"

She guessed where this was going. "Thanks to me, it's not," she interrupted.

"—so why not make up for yesterday and spend time with your little whippersnapper," Gus finished kindly.

Hannah could tell him why not. "There are still a lot of new items to be priced and shelved."

"Marcy and I can do that," Valerie said. "Seriously. We'll get that done this morning and if there are any problems with the installation this afternoon…"

"They can call me," Gus said.

"And I'll drive him over there," Ruthann volunteered.

"Wait a minute. Today is supposed to be your day off," Hannah said to Ruthann. Since turning sixty, Ruthann had scaled back to a four-day work week. And she still got more done in four days than most young people did in five.

"And I'm still taking it. I'm going back to my house to make preserves with the last of the summer peach crop. And your dad is going to help me."

Hannah looked at him. Irritation creased his white brow. "I can measure sugar and pectin and stir a pot with one hand."

Gus had never even helped her mother in the kitchen!

What was happening to him? Was he getting mellow in his golden years? Or had Isabella's presence brought out a renewed appreciation of life in him, too? All Hannah knew for certain was that everyone in the kitchen was looking at her, waiting for her to do what they considered the right thing in this instance.

"You're not going to get this chance to play hooky every day," Ruthann persisted.

Hannah looked at Joe. "I guess I could proofread those pages for you." She really needed to mark that off her to-do list, anyway.

"The pages can wait," Joe said firmly, setting a plateful of blueberry-and-oatmeal pancakes in front of her. "A little R and R cannot."

AN HOUR LATER, HANNAH ADMITTED everyone was right. It felt good to put on a pair of old jeans and a T-shirt, and just hang out at home for a change, her only agenda spending time with her daughter.

Joe appeared in the doorway of the nursery. Like her, he'd showered and put on comfortably broken-in clothing. He smelled of soap, mint mouthwash and man.

Looking impossibly sexy and relaxed, he strode to the edge of the quilt Hannah had put down on the center of the nursery rug. "What's going on here?"

"Unfortunately, nothing yet," Hannah replied.

Joe stretched out on the other side of Isabella who was lying on her tummy, head raised ever so slightly, studying the brightly colored alphabet-letter appliqués.

Joe's eyes danced. "What's supposed to be going on?"

"Tummy time. I'm trying to get her interested in learning to crawl. But all she wants to do is look at the fabric."

Joe noticed the ring of baby toys placed in a half circle

around Isabella's upper body. He smoothed a hand across the fabric with the same deft touch he'd used when they had made love. "I can see why. It's a pretty quilt."

"My mom made it for me when I was a kid and saved it for my children."

His expression turned tender. "It must be nice to have so much history."

Seizing the opportunity to get closer to him emotionally, Hannah asked casually, "Your parents didn't make anything for you?"

A mixture of regret and acceptance tightened his handsome features. "It wasn't their style. They used to bring me souvenirs from their various adventures around the world, though. A samovar from Russia, silk cap from China, a wood carving from South America."

Dividing her attention equally between the two, Hannah moved a toy closer to Isabella. "Where do you keep that stuff?"

Joe watched as Isabella dropped her head to the quilt, then determinedly pushed it back up again. "In a trunk in the attic at my aunt and uncle's."

"You don't have a home base anywhere. An apartment you keep?" Hannah asked, amazed.

Joe shook his head. "I'm always traveling."

Hannah blinked. "Even holidays?"

"Especially holidays." Joe paused and looked at her. "You don't approve?"

Hannah shrugged but did not look away. "It just sounds lonely."

Briefly, sadness permeated his low tone. "Lonely is being where you don't belong when you want to belong. Traveling on a holiday is nothing. You just get lost in the crowd of other people trying to get lost in the crowd."

Her heart going out to him, Hannah said, "I couldn't live that way."

"I know."

Silence fell between them, more awkward now.

"So what do you say we get this show on the road?" Joe shifted around so he was facing the top of Isabella's head. He began coaxing her quietly in Mandarin Chinese.

She lifted her head, fixed her dark eyes on his face and smiled, but made absolutely no effort to move or grasp any of the toys Hannah had put out for her. Joe spoke to her some more. Wiggled a toy in front of her. Again, nothing.

He sat up. "Maybe if we demonstrate what we want her to do…?"

"I already tried that," Hannah confessed, laughing. "Didn't work." She sat up, stretching her legs out straight in front of her, then picked up Isabella and laid her sideways, the baby's chest across her thighs. She guided Isabella's arms out in front of her, until they slanted down toward the floor. "But one of the books said this might work."

Sure enough, Isabella began to squirm a little. Most likely, Hannah decided, because it wasn't all that comfortable a position.

Hannah tried again, using a rolled-up bath towel as a tummy pillow for her daughter. Isabella didn't particularly like it, either.

Hannah sat her up on her lap and handed her a toy. Isabella grasped it and promptly moved it to her mouth, content to play.

Joe stayed where he was, stretched out on his side, head propped on his hand, looking as concerned as any father. "How do babies usually learn to crawl?" he asked curiously.

Wishing for what seemed the millionth time that he were Isabella's daddy, Hannah replied, "The books say they get up on all fours, and then rock back and forth until they inch forward a little bit. Once they get the hang of that, or experience even a little success, they take off. The trick is getting them to start reaching for things when they are on their tummies. Equally important is developing the strength to sit up on their own."

"She seems to be doing pretty well with that," Joe observed proudly.

Hannah smiled, as Isabella leaned forward and touched her toes with one hand. The toy still pressed to her mouth, she worked on pulling her sock off her foot.

"What are you doing the rest of the day?" Hannah laughed as Isabella freed her toes, wiggling and exploring them intently.

Watching, Joe chuckled, too. He leaned over to press a kiss to the bottom of Isabella's bare foot. "That's what I came in to ask. How would the two of you feel about accompanying me on a picture-taking expedition?"

JOE WASN'T KIDDING WHEN HE'D said he wanted to take photos for his travel guide on the Trans-Pecos region of Texas. The three of them spent the rest of the day getting in and out of his SUV, taking photos of canyons, desolate fence posts, diners and gas stations out in the middle of nowhere. Hannah loved every minute of it, and so did Isabella. But by the time she had Isabella tucked into bed for the night, she knew she had to get serious about her *own* professional responsibilities.

So Hannah asked Valerie if she would mind babysitting her sleeping daughter while she went down to the Mercantile to check out the finished carpentry and newly installed plumbing to the coffee and ice-cream soda bar.

"Sure thing."

Joe stood. "I'll tag along. Give you a hand."

Hannah's heartbeat picked up. "You sure?" He'd already put in a full day.

Joe nodded, already reaching for his SUV keys. "With the two of us, it will go twice as fast."

Gus, who was exhausted from a day spent with Ruthann, yawned. "I won't wait up," he said.

"Please don't," Hannah replied. "I want you getting your rest."

"And I want you," he said, right back, "to get yourself a husband."

Aware her father was only half-kidding, she rolled her eyes. "Good night, Dad. See you in the morning."

Minutes later, they walked in the front door of the Mercantile and switched on the overhead lights.

Hannah smiled approvingly, noting all the work that had been done that day. Groceries geared for tourists were toward the front of the left half of the store. Cowboy grub like canned meats, beans and biscuit mix was toward the center. Portable high-energy foods for campers were located on the right, opposite the old-fashioned saloon-style coffee and ice-cream soda bar. The carpenters had done a great job hiding the new coffeemakers in the custom-built armoire. The freezer case, for the ice cream, was located just inside the bar and was also hidden from view. "This looks so much nicer than I imagined it would." Hannah ran a hand across the distressed mahogany finish of the bar.

Joe agreed. "What's going there?" He pointed to a big empty square of floor in the center of the store.

Hannah grinned. "My faux camping site, complete with fake tree."

"Yeah?"

"Want to help set it up?" she asked, as excited about this as she was the rest of the changes she was making.

"Sure."

Together, they brought out all the gear. Together, they spread an evergreen rug over the distressed wood plank floor. While Joe worked on putting up the two-person tent, Hannah set out two canvas folding chairs, battery-operated lamp and stove. She propped two fishing rods against a tackle box and positioned hiking boots and backpacks against a fake tree.

"Want the flaps open or shut?" he asked, standing back to admire his handiwork.

Hannah studied the tableau with a critical eye. "Probably leave one open and one shut. But first, I have to put these sleeping bags in there."

She got down on her hands and knees, kicked off her boots and crawled inside. She unrolled the bags, placed them side by side and then sat back. "What do you think?" she asked over her shoulder, waving him closer. "Should I leave them like this? Or open them both up and put one on the bottom and then zip the other one overtop of it, so it looks like it's a double bed?"

Joe stuck his head in the tent to better assess the setup. "You're the marketing exec. Who's the two-person tent targeted to sell to—kids on a sleep-out or adults looking for a little romance?"

"Good question." She frowned, thinking. "I guess I'll try it the other way, since adults with kids will probably want one of the bigger family-size tents."

Joe disappeared.

She stuck her head back out, pointed. "Would you mind handing me those pillows?"

Joe passed them in. Hannah put them down, then stretched out on her back and looked up at the top of the tent.

"Now what are you doing?" Joe asked in an amused voice.

She sighed, feeling more perplexed than ever. "I'm trying to figure out if this is the size tent that should be on display in here. I figured we'd go with the two-person tent because that was the one we were most likely to sell a lot of, statistically."

Joe went down on one knee to converse more comfortably. "It seemed a little claustrophobic when I first got in, but it looks cozy enough now."

"With just me inside," Hannah allowed. "If you were to get in…it might be a little crowded."

Joe's brows furrowed. "I don't think so."

"Let's find out. Take your shoes off and come on in."

He climbed in after her, stretched out and promptly proved true what Hannah had suspected. He was so big he took up over half the interior. Worse, even with his head pressed against the rear wall of the tent, his feet stuck out the front flaps a good four or five inches.

Hannah groaned and slapped a palm against her forehead in aggravation. "I can't believe I was so stupid!"

Joe shifted so he could look at her.

"I was so sure I was going to sell a ton of these things with the great fall weather coming up, that I took the deep discount the sales rep offered me and preordered a hundred of these five-foot by six-foot tents." Hannah shook her head and grimaced. "I'll never be able to sell them all. My dad is never going to let me live it down. Especially after the way I acted about his overordering of the campfire beans."

"You were very gracious and subtle about the campfire beans thing, and as for these tents, I'm sure the sales statistics have accurately predicted what you can expect."

Regretfully, she explained, "They were national figures, Joe. They didn't take into account how tall the men in Texas are, compared to other parts of the country. A guy like you who is over six feet tall would never be able to sleep in this thing."

"Sure I could," he vowed.

"Not comfortably," Hannah argued. "Not with someone else."

"Maybe not with someone I wasn't romantically interested in," Joe cautioned, already wrapping an arm around her waist. "But if we were a couple, and you turned onto your side, and I curled up against you, like this—" he pulled her backward, until she was flush against him in the small intimate confines of the tent "—we'd be snug as two bugs in a rug."

Hannah caught her breath at the feel of him, so warm and solid, pressed up against her. Was it her imagination or was he…?

"Yeah, but if we tried to sleep side by side on our backs…" Ignoring the way her tummy was fluttering in anticipation, Hannah extricated herself from his embrace and turned.

He turned, too.

"We wouldn't even be able to shut the flaps and be all in," she finished breathlessly.

"Sure we could." Joe sat up, brought the flaps down and lay back down again. He flattened his feet on the floor of the tent, bent his knees slightly and folded his arms behind his head. "See?" he said.

Hannah didn't know whether to laugh or cry over the magnitude of her business mistake. The only thing she was sure about was that she was way too aware of Joe Daugherty. "You're just trying to make me feel better," she claimed.

"If I wanted to do that," Joe said, framing her face with his hands and draping her with his body, "then I would do…this."

Chapter Twelve

Hannah had been aching for Joe for what seemed like forever. So the moment his lips touched hers was like receiving manna from heaven. Intense need burst through her at the speed of light.

He nipped at the bottom of her lip, feasting on it. "I thought we weren't going to do this again," he teased, threading his fingers through her hair.

Remembering just how much she had been thinking about seducing Joe—at least in theory—Hannah allowed her body to quicken in return. "That was the plan," she allowed. Although it seemed he was getting ahead of her in the taking-charge department.

He shifted onto his side, freeing her. Something dark and seductive flashed in his green eyes. "Then…?"

She rolled onto her side, so they were facing each other. Unbuttoning his shirt, she admired the hard male contours of his chest. His body heated beneath her touch. Lower still, she felt that familiar hardness pressing against her. "You're right," she breathed, pressing hot kisses across his collarbone. The taste of his skin lingered on her tongue. She moaned softly, even as she cursed her unexpected boldness.

"This really…really…has to be the last time." For both of their sakes.

He shifted, pressing closer, until she could feel the hard demanding length of him against her much softer frame. He kissed the side of her neck and the shell of her ear, before stealing between her lips once again. "And why is that?"

She stirred, feeling incredibly beautiful and sensual beneath his touch. Helpless to resist, she lifted her arms as he peeled off her top and bra, and undid the zipper on her jeans. She raised herself slightly as they, too, came off, followed swiftly by her socks and thong.

"Because if we keep making love like this, I'm not going to want you to leave Summit," she murmured, helping him get naked, too.

"As if I'm going to want to go," he muttered between sweet, sipping kisses. Cupping her breasts with his hands, he laved her nipples with his tongue.

Hannah reveled in the rush of pleasure, and the incredible feeling of anticipation. "But you have to."

Joe worked his way down her body, stroking and exploring. Hannah closed her eyes, letting the luxuriant sensations wash over her.

The feel of his evening beard chafing her skin. The soft, wet warmth of his mouth. His hands, at once rough and tender. The knowledge she was being adored and possessed, all at once. The need to feel love and love in return welled inside her. Hannah arched against him, knowing even if it didn't last, this was right…so right…

"I'm not…leaving…yet…. We have this time," he told her gruffly as he parted her thighs, and the last little grain of her resistance dissolved.

And, Joe thought, it was time he intended to take.

Not because he was what she needed…long-term. But because he was what she needed and wanted here and now. Because he had never felt like this before. Never been with a woman who was everything to him. Never felt like he wouldn't exist without her.

Until now, sex for him had been just…well, sex. With Hannah it was different. Something more. Something special. Something unique to him and to her.

When he touched her, she melted into him. When she touched him, he burned with an inner heat that was so possessive he knew he would do everything for her. In return, all he wanted was to feel her arms and legs wrapped around him, the softness of her body arching, opening, drawing him in, deep.

He wanted to taste her mouth and feel her heat, and experience the way she pressed against him, so sweet and womanly, even as she urged him on. Harder. Hotter. Until there was nothing in the world, nothing left, but the two of them and this incredible passion that would not be denied.

"WELL, THAT WAS A MISTAKE," Hannah declared afterward.

The two of them lay on their backs, still struggling to catch their breath.

Joe turned and surveyed her with lazy pleasure. Hannah was deliciously tousled. Naked. And his. All his. At least for the moment. "For two people trying to be just friends, you're not kidding—that was the wrong tact to take," he quipped. He ran a hand playfully through her hair, loving the fragrance and silky feel of it.

She grinned at the irony in his low tone and with the tips of her fingers, traced the contours of his chest. "It felt amazing, nevertheless."

Joe's body responded, as she had to have known it would.

Aware he hadn't had his fill of her, he nudged her knees apart and settled between them. "So amazing, in fact," he drawled, dropping kisses over her soft damp skin. He smiled at her quiet gasp of pleasure, knowing if he had his way, she wouldn't be restrained for long. "I'm tempted to do it all over again."

Hannah trembled, a mixture of excitement and anticipation in her pretty sable-brown eyes. "This really has to be the last time."

He did not want to think beyond the moment. "That being the case," he murmured, thinking of the many ways to please her, "I'll do whatever you want as much as you want." Whatever it took, he thought, to make their lovemaking last and last and last....

Hannah's hips came up to meet him. "Exactly the problem...." She gasped, holding his head in her hands, and blessedly letting him have his way with her. "Exactly what makes you so very hard to resist."

And she wasn't the only one who got everything she wanted and more. As the evening wore on, Hannah proved herself as skilled a lover as she was everything else. Tempting, teasing. Knowing exactly what to do and when to do it. Leading him to the kind of finish he hadn't known possible. Surprising him after that, by once again, pulling away. And this time, getting dressed.

Aware she had a baby to get home to, and a babysitter who just might be getting curious, Joe reluctantly shrugged on his clothes, too. "You meant what you said, didn't you?" His throat felt tight. He stepped out of the tent and looked her in the eye. "About this being the last time we make love?"

Hannah picked up the sleeping bags they'd broken in, and replaced them with two brand-new ones. "Don't you see?" She gave him the answer he did not want to hear as she knelt and rolled the bags up. "It has to be. What we've had here is so good…"

Joe studied her. "You don't want to ruin it with any messy goodbyes."

"Right. I want us to stay friends. I want you to continue to be a part of Isabella's life. And mine. And I'm afraid—" she drew a trembling breath before she met his gaze once more "—if we let ourselves pretend…even for a moment…that this could be something more than exactly what it is, that we won't part friends, in the end."

Disappointment surged through him. Like everyone else in his life he'd become close to, she already had one foot out the door. Joe told himself he wasn't surprised. He had known all along he wasn't the kind of guy people got emotionally attached to, or invited into their world, long-term. There was always a reason. An excuse. A way that let both parties exit gracefully.

Figuring if either of them should pay for the no-longer-good-as-new camping gear, it should be him, he opened up his wallet and withdrew his credit card. "You're right. I don't want either of us to be hurt, either."

His action added another level of cool practicality to the situation. She hesitated only briefly before reaching for the card. She stood there, holding it in her palm, looking up at him. "So you agree—tonight is the last time?"

Reluctantly, yeah. Joe forced himself to be the Texas gentleman she needed him to be. "I won't make another move," he told her calmly. And this time it would be a promise he was going to have to keep because he didn't think he could make love to her again and stay "just friends." "And I'll take the sleeping bags." He watched her walk over to the cashier's counter and run the card through the machine. "They're something I don't have and can use." Something, he thought with unexpected sentimentality, to remember this night by.

Again, Hannah hesitated. Briefly, she looked as torn as he felt. "You're sure?" she asked, as if to a customer who was on the fence about a purchase. Her elegant brow furrowed as she waited for his reply.

Joe nodded reluctantly. The two sleeping bags weren't much, as far as a memento, but they were something. "Absolutely," he said.

"SO WHAT'S LEFT TO DO BEFORE we reopen tomorrow?" Gus asked Hannah Sunday afternoon, when they all gathered at the Mercantile for one last push.

Hannah consulted the list on her clipboard, while Joe propped a drowsy Isabella against him. Trying not to think how perfect a father he would make, if he ever decided to take the plunge and become one, Hannah turned her attention to the task at hand. "The new soda glasses need to be washed and shelved."

"I'll handle that," Marcy said.

Isabella's head dropped to Joe's broad shoulder. She yawned sleepily, rubbed her eyes with her fist, and then cuddled even closer into the hard warmth of his chest.

I've really got to stop noticing how cute they look together, Hannah thought, or how inseparable they had become. Joe was just spending so much time with Isabella today because he knew his chances to do so were dwindling precariously. Labor Day was a week from tomorrow. He had already said he was leaving Summit the day after that. And attending the Lights Festival in Marfa for a few days before that. Which meant, he had what—five or six days to actually spend with them—days when he wouldn't be otherwise occupied or off somewhere else.

Hannah had known this moment was coming. Had been reminded of it in some way every day. Yet the thought of Joe leaving was enough to bring a lump to her throat and tears to her eyes. Which was why, she schooled herself sternly, she had to stop thinking about it, stop wishing the situation were different, and just enjoy each moment of each day as it came. The way they had last night.

That was the only way she would survive.

The only way they would remain friends, and she did want to stay at least that.

Aware everyone was waiting for her to continue, Hannah cleared her throat and continued reading over the list of chores she had drawn up. "The beverage menu needs to be put on the chalkboard, before we mount it on the wall behind the bar."

"I can do that in calligraphy," Ruthann volunteered.

Hannah moved to the next item. "Someone needs to set up the new coffee machines and make sure they are all working."

"That, I can do," Valerie enthused, drawing on her previous experience as a barista at a campus coffee shop.

"We've got a new box of insulated travel mugs that we need priced and shelved."

"I'll handle that," Gus said.

Joe lifted a quizzical brow as all eyes turned to him. Hannah felt another surge of emotion as she saw the way her daughter was clinging to Joe, and the tender way he was holding Isabella in return. They really were going to miss each other, too.

Hannah forced herself to smile before she burst into sentimental tears. "You just keep on doing what you're doing until our little darlin' falls asleep and we can put her in her playpen for a nap," she said.

Joe nodded.

While everyone else got started, Hannah went to the storeroom to hunt for the boxes of premium coffee with Valerie. After ten minutes, Valerie threw up her hands in frustration. "This is…"

"A disorganized mess," Hannah said. "I know. I'm going to take care of that this afternoon so we can find what we need a lot more quickly." Hannah shifted aside boxes of five- by six-foot tents that were going to have to go back to the manufacturer, and kept looking.

Finally, Valerie located the coffee boxes. Hannah joined in helping her open them up.

They were just walking out of the storeroom, when the bell over the front door jingled. It was followed by a low murmur of voices.

Instantly, the color drained from Valerie's face. "Oh, no," she whispered, a hand to her mouth.

"What?" Hannah said, perplexed.

"You'll see soon enough," Valerie muttered with a disgruntled frown.

As the two of them walked out onto the sales floor of the Mercantile, Joe passed them, a sound asleep Isabella on his shoulder.

Motioning them to silence with a finger to his lips he aimed a sympathetic glance Valerie's way and slipped into the office to settle Isabella into her playpen.

"…we're not open for business today," Marcy was telling the well-dressed couple standing just inside the front doors.

It didn't take long for Hannah to figure out who they were. The man had the same burnished-gold hair and intense green eyes as Joe and Valerie. The familial resemblance between the three Daughertys was unmistakable.

"We're not here to buy anything," said the trim, sophisticated woman in the satin blouse and flowing trousers. She laid her hand over the expensive jewelry around her neck. "We're here to take our daughter back to school!"

Silence reigned in the store. Joe returned to the tense scene, and looked from his aunt and uncle to his cousin.

Gus motioned to Marcy and Ruthann to step outside on the front porch of the Mercantile, and give the Daugherty family some privacy.

Thinking it a good idea, Hannah moved to follow suit.

Valerie grabbed Hannah's arm. "I want you and Joe to stay," she said fiercely.

Reluctantly, Hannah complied.

Once their audience was diminished, Valerie wasted no time squaring off with her folks. "I'm not going back with you."

"You need to finish your education," Karl Daugherty said.

"I've already applied to transfer to Texas Tech and I've been accepted for spring semester. I'll finish my last year there and graduate next August."

"We want you to finish your degree where you started it," Karl said.

Valerie shook her head defiantly. "No way."

Camille glared at her daughter. "Chris has been patient thus far, but there is a limit to how much he will endure. And Professor Hamilton has pulled every string it's possible to pull to keep you in the program."

"First of all, Professor Hamilton is not doing that for me. She's doing that to protect herself, and possibly Chris. And second of all, there's a limit to how much I'll endure, too. And I'm not walking in to find the two of them in flagrante ever again!"

The revelation sent a stunned hush over the room. Camille clutched her jewelry even more tightly. "My heavens! You're saying…?"

"Professor Hamilton and Chris have been having an

affair. I know, because I walked into his apartment and found them together in his bed and there was no doubt about what was going on."

Camille gasped, looking all the more upset. "She's married! With children!"

"And twenty years older than he is," Valerie continued sarcastically, hurt and disillusionment reverberating in her low tone. Angry tears filled her eyes. "Not that this seems to matter to either of them. They think that because they're both consenting adults, and he wasn't a student in any of her classes, that it's okay. And that it was okay for her to mentor me—not because she was interested in me as a student, or wanted to further my love of English literature, but because she wanted to get close enough to seduce my too-hot-for-his-own-good boyfriend. And if you say one word about what a fine family he is from, or what a bright political future he is likely to have one day, I really will be sick."

Her parents stared at her, clearly mortified. "Why didn't you tell us any of this sooner?" Karl demanded.

Surely, Hannah thought, they would have understood.

"Because it was humiliating!" Valerie cried, even more distraught. "And I was embarrassed!" The tears she had been holding back began to fall. "The whole mess makes me look like such a loser!"

"You're not a loser," Hannah and Joe interjected passionately in unison.

Karl and Camille sent aggravated looks at them both for interrupting, then turned back to their daughter. "Obviously, we're very disappointed in Chris and in Professor Hamilton," her father said, "but you did nothing wrong. You can still go back to the university and hold your head high and finish your education."

Valerie scoffed at the idea. "And have people talking about me behind my back the whole time?" she countered, even more emotionally. "I don't think so." She paused to dash away her tears with the back of her hand. "I'm getting out of that fishbowl and taking the semester off. And I'm doing it whether you approve or not! I have a job here, in a community I love, and I even have a place to stay for the next six months." Valerie looked at Hannah and held up her palm. "Don't worry. I'm not freeloading at your place forever. I've already talked to the landlord and signed a lease on the cabin Joe is renting. I'll move in as soon as Joe moves out next week."

The reminder that Joe really was leaving hit Hannah like a blow to the solar plexus.

"Now, if you'll excuse me," Valerie told her parents stonily, "I'm working here." Valerie turned on her heel and headed for the storeroom.

Camille waited until her daughter was out of earshot, then looked at Joe. "Please talk some sense into your cousin. Get her to come back with us in time to start the fall semester next week."

Joe refused with a brief shake of his head. "It's her decision. I respect her right to make it. Although, for the record, I think she's doing the right thing in walking away from what has to be an exceedingly uncomfortable situation. If I were her, I wouldn't go back to that mess, either."

"And what would you have her become—a wanderer like you?" Camille cried emotionally. "A person who never actually commits to anything or anyone?"

Karl turned to Camille. "Joe is plenty committed to his writing career."

"But nothing else!" Camille snapped.

Joe winced at the truth in his aunt's assertion.

Before the situation could deteriorate further, Karl tried again, more reasonably. "Valerie listens to you, Joe. If you tell her to pull herself together, stop hiding out here and return to school like the sophisticated young woman she is, then she will."

Sensing what Joe's response was going to be, Camille added unkindly, "We know you've always been 'different' than the rest of us, Joe. And we put up with you all these years, but you need to understand something. If you don't help us out here, you will not be welcome in our home. You'll be out of the family."

Karl's scowl said he agreed.

Joe shrugged. "Then I'm out."

"And so," Valerie said, walking right back in, "am I."

"Obviously, you don't mean that," Karl told his daughter, a stricken look on his face.

"Obviously, I do," Valerie insisted. It was clear from the look on her face that she had heard everything. "If you disown Joe, I'm gone, too."

Joe turned to Valerie. "You don't have to do that," he told her firmly, looking as if he had expected this to happen one day all along. "It's okay. They're right," he said with a shrug. "I never belonged. There's no reason," he finished, making no effort to disguise his bitterness, "to keep pretending otherwise."

"ARE YOU OKAY?" VALERIE ASKED Joe when they'd gone back to organize the storeroom, after her parents had left in a huff.

Joe followed Hannah's direction and moved several cartons of granola over to the section now designated for "breakfast" foods. "Isn't that the question I'm supposed to be asking you?" he mused, relieved to see his cousin so composed after her big blowup with her parents.

Valerie located the pancake and waffle mixes, and brought those over, too. "I'm fine."

To Joe's continued surprise, she looked more at peace than she had since she had arrived in Summit.

Valerie went back to get the cartons of maple syrup. "I'm tired of being pushed into things that I know in my gut are wrong for me."

Hannah pushed a dolly full of oatmeal over to them. "Like your relationship with Chris Elliott?" she guessed sympathetically.

Valerie sighed. "The truth is, I've had plenty of time to think about that in the last few weeks. I think we probably would have broken up a long time ago if Mom and Dad hadn't liked him so much. They keep saying they want me to marry somebody who is 'going places.' The truth of the matter is, I prefer guys—and a life—that is much more laid-back."

"Like Summit?" Joe remarked.

Valerie nodded. "I'm thinking about coming back here permanently to live, once I get my degree next summer. That is—" she turned to her employer "—if I'll still have a job at the Mercantile."

"You'll always have a job here," Hannah said. "Perhaps one with much more responsibility."

"Fantastic!" Valerie beamed.

"Your parents aren't going to like that, either," Joe advised.

Valerie shrugged off the warning and went back to moving stacked items around until they were in alphabetical order, by section. "I'm sure Mom and Dad would much prefer me to settle down in a place that is a lot less out of the way. But like I said, I like a much quieter life and it is time I stepped out on my own."

Joe worried about the long-term impact of her actions, however sensible they seemed to her now. "Just don't let the tension go on between you and your folks for too long, okay?"

Valerie's expression darkened. "I meant what I said, Joe. If Mom and Dad cut you out of the family, then I'm cutting them out."

He stopped what he was doing and walked over to his cousin. He wrapped an arm about her shoulders in a brief fraternal hug. "I appreciate you going to bat for me, kid," he said gruffly, more touched by her devotion to him than he could say. He drew back to look at her. "But I also know that we only get one set of parents and for better or worse, Aunt Camille and Uncle Karl are yours and they love you."

Valerie studied Joe, tears glittering in her eyes. "They just don't love you," she concluded hoarsely.

Joe shook off the emotion that threatened to engulf him, too. For both their sake's, he stated carefully, "I think they've done their best to deal with a responsibility they never wanted and never should have had. The point is I am an adult." He gave Valerie another reassuring hug. "You and I will always be family to each other, even if I'm not family to them. And you should be close with the rest of your family, too. You shouldn't have to choose between the two of us. Because that isn't right."

Valerie's lower lip trembled. "It's so unfair. I just don't get why they don't love you."

"I don't get it, either," Hannah said, after Valerie had hugged Joe one last time and gone out onto the floor to see if she could get the new coffeemakers all set up.

Joe hefted boxes off the dolly, onto shelving. "Love isn't something you can order up on demand, Hannah."

Looking incredibly beautiful with her hair swept up into a tousled knot on the back of her head, she shot him a wry glance. "That's not what people told me when I was petitioning to adopt."

Joe did his best to comfort Hannah, too. "Sometimes it doesn't happen," he told her softly. "The connection is just not there. People have to deal with that and move on with their lives." The way he had.

Hannah raked her teeth across her bottom lip. "I don't know if I could be as accepting."

Desire stirred inside him. Aware how very much he wanted to make love to her, Joe continued softly, "Heaven willing, you'll never have to find out."

As they looked at each other, the connection between the two of them intensified. "You're such a good guy, so kind and loving, I don't know how I am ever going to say goodbye to you," Hannah murmured emotionally.

Joe didn't know how he was going to pack up and go, either, and he didn't want to waste time thinking about it. "Fortunately, we don't have to do that just yet," he told her cheerfully, forcing himself to concentrate on the positive. He closed the distance between the two of them in two lazy strides, sifted his hands through her hair and tilted her face up to his. "We still have another week to spend together. So what do you say we make the most of the time we have left?"

Chapter Thirteen

"I don't know about you, but I think we may very well be victims of a conspiracy here," Hannah told Joe Thursday evening when they once again found themselves quite alone, now that Isabella had been put down for the evening.

Gus and Ruthann had gone to her house to watch television. Valerie was out with friends she had made since arriving in Summit.

"Definitely matchmaking in the air," Joe agreed.

"Too bad they're going to be disappointed in the end." Steeling herself against further heartache, Hannah pulled a load of laundry out of the dryer.

A corner of his mouth lifted. "Because you're not going to leave everything behind and go with me to Australia?" he asked wryly.

"And you're not going to chuck everything and stay?" For both their sakes, she adapted the same light and easy tone.

They grinned at each other. Knowing, even if no one else did, that there were no easy solutions to their situation.

Joe leaned against the portal, arms crossed in front of him. "There is something we could do, however," he drawled.

"And what," Hannah asked, her mouth already dry, her

heart pounding, "would that be?" She knew what she hoped. Even if it was one of the worst ideas ever. She wanted to make love again. One last time…for the road, for posterity, for memories…

Oblivious to the decidedly licentious nature of her thoughts, Joe edged closer. He looked down into her face, serious now. "You know I have to go to Marfa this weekend, for the Lights Festival."

Hannah nodded. She not only knew, she had been dreading his departure, more than she could say.

"The hotels in the area are fully booked. Have been for months. But I've got a room with two queen-size beds and room for a port-a-crib."

Two beds. As in separate "I am not going to sleep with you again" accommodations. With difficulty, Hannah swallowed around the parched feeling in her throat. Determined to play it as cool as he was, she plastered an easygoing smile on her face. "Are you asking me to go with you?" she asked sweetly.

Joe shrugged a broad shoulder in his usual affable manner. "Could be fun," he said in a deep lazy voice that wreaked havoc with her insides. And this time he did not move closer to her, but instead wisely kept his distance. "There's live music, and lots of food, and of course an exploration of the famous Marfa Lights to be had."

Hannah knew, she had been to the festival many times as a kid, with her mom and dad.

Joe's gaze drifted lazily over her face before returning to her eyes. "It'd be a chance to kick back and have a good time, and have one last hurrah together before I leave Summit. So…" A heartbeat passed, then another and another. "What do you say? Will you and Isabella go with me?"

HANNAH THOUGHT ABOUT the invitation the rest of the evening, and all the next day, while she alternately waited on customers and worked out a deal with the camping gear manufacturer to swap out the tents she had ordered for a larger size, without her father being any the wiser about her embarrassing mistake.

But Joe was always in her thoughts. His proposition tempting her even as it scared her away.

On the one hand, she was happy he respected her decision to just be friends and not lovers anymore. On the other hand, she was disappointed because the quick way he had backed off could only mean that their lovemaking had not been nearly as thrilling to him as it had been to her. And that was a bummer. She'd thought…hoped…that she had turned him on every bit as much as he had turned her on. Obviously, that wasn't the case.

Which made it easier for them both to behave sensibly. Joe was already close to breaking her heart. If they made love again…

Well, they just wouldn't, Hannah promised herself matter-of-factly. That didn't mean, however, they couldn't still have a good time together before he left town. And by late Friday afternoon, she knew what she wanted to do. All she had to do was figure out a way to make it happen. The first person she went to speak with was her father, who had dropped by to see how things were going. She caught up with him in the Mercantile office, going over the receipts for the first five days after reopening. He was smiling broadly at the totals.

Hannah beamed with pride. She knew this was just the beginning of the turnaround. Although she didn't expect him to admit that to her just yet. "Hey, Dad. I heard you were here."

"I saw you helping a customer pick out camping gear. You really know your stuff."

"I've been studying up on it. Listen." Hannah came all the way into the office. For the first time she felt like she and her dad were on equal footing, professionally. It felt good. "You know how I told you I didn't want you overdoing it at the Mercantile anymore?"

Gus looked up. For the first time, there was no fight in his expression. "Yes."

"Well, that still holds." Hannah knew she sounded like a mother hen. Or maybe just a mother, period. She didn't care. She could no more stop the nurturing vibes coming out of her than she could halt her heartbeat. "You cannot be here all day every day anymore."

Gus leaned back in the creaky wooden desk chair that was nearly as old as the store. Hannah made a mental note to have that replaced for something a lot more comfortable.

Gus exhaled. "What's your point?"

This, Hannah thought, was the slightly embarrassing part. "Uh…. How do you feel about being on call, to handle emergencies that might come up either in person or by phone?"

Gus grinned, irritation fading as quickly as it had appeared. "You want to go to Marfa with Joe, don't you?"

He might as well have been chanting, "Hannah and Joe, sitting in a tree, *k-i-s-s-i-n-g*."

Hannah blushed but forged on, anyway. "I'm that transparent, hmm?"

"What do you think, hotshot?" Gus rocked back in his chair, a smug smile on his weathered face. "And for the record, I'd be happy to cover for you."

"I'll assist," Ruthann said, popping in.

She was soon joined by the other eavesdropper on the

premises. "I don't mind working all weekend, either," Valerie said. "I need the extra money for the deposit for the cabin."

"Thanks—everyone," Hannah said. "I owe you."

"What about this little one?" Gus asked, as Joe walked in with Isabella in his arms. "Is she staying here or going with you and Joe?"

Realizing what Hannah's answer to his invitation was, Joe's face brightened. "This little darlin' is definitely going with her mama and me," he said, pausing to kiss the top of Isabella's head. "We need our time together before I hit the road again."

"You know they don't think you're really leaving," Hannah said an hour later, as she and Joe finished packing and headed out to his SUV.

Joe put the bags in the back, while Hannah settled Isabella into her car seat.

"Then they'd be wrong." Joe looked at Hannah over the hood of the vehicle, his expression suddenly serious. A heartbeat passed. Then he asked quietly, "Does that change your mind?"

Hannah shook her head. Her mind was made up. "No. I want this time together, too," she whispered. Because the end of their journey was coming all too soon.

"So what's your opinion?" Joe asked a couple of hours later, as the two of them sat in his SUV, looking out over the plain, along with countless other festival-goers. Isabella slept soundly in her car seat in the back.

The circular adobe viewing station was nearby. Because it was packed with tourists angling to get a view, Hannah and Joe had pulled off the road and parked a short distance away on the plain. This afforded them a good view of the vast Mitchell Flat and the Chinati mountain range. A full moon shone overhead, adding extra illumination across the vast Texas landscape. They were almost a mile high, yet they were in the desert. The combination of unlikely elements gave the night an eerie, almost otherworldly aura. Hannah found herself shivering in the cool evening air, wafting in through the windows. She turned to check on Isabella, then they slipped wordlessly out of the vehicle to stand against the front grill of Joe's Land Rover.

Joe checked out the landscape with his night vision glasses. "So what do you think?" His voice was a sexy rumble in the nocturnal silence. "Are we going to see the mysterious Marfa Lights tonight or not?"

Hannah chuckled and looked out over the plain. Even without binoculars she could make out a trio of faint white lights, pulsing and dimming. "Check those out—right over there."

"Those definitely aren't car lights."

"Or motorcycles," Hannah murmured, watching the playful bounce and spin of the distant dancing orbs.

Joe handed over the night goggles. "I'd heard they were colored."

Hannah looked through the lenses, amazed at how much clearer the lights appeared. "Sometimes they are," she said, frowning as the lights faded, and then disappeared, without warning.

She sighed and handed the goggles back to Joe.

He looped the strand holding the night glasses around his neck and then looked over at her. "Have you ever seen colored ones?"

Hannah brushed the hair out of her face. Thinking she should have brought a warmer wrap for herself, she stuck her hands in the pockets of her denim jacket. "Oh, yeah, plenty of times."

Joe, who had no jacket to give her, circled his arm around her and warmed her with his body heat. "When?"

Hannah kept her eyes on the distant plain, hoping to see the mysterious lights again. "When I was a teenager."

Joe chuckled. "Let me guess. This was a prime parking spot."

"Well…yes. It still is, when the festival isn't going on and there aren't so many tourists. Whoa. Did you see that?"

"Was it red?"

"Orange, I thought."

"And there's one that's…blue."

"Yeah." Cuddled into the curve of his body, Hannah stared into the distance with him. "That didn't last long," she said, disappointed.

They watched a while longer. In the SUV, Isabella continued to sleep contentedly. "Supposedly, people have been seeing the lights since the nineteenth century," Hannah said.

Joe nodded. "Which sort of disabuses one of the current theories being bandied about by college kids—that the mysterious lights are really car lights on U.S. 67. Since they didn't have cars back then."

"Or UFO's," Hannah joked, as another strong gust of wind blew across the desert.

Joe moved to block the chill. He carefully tucked an errant strand of her hair behind her ear. "Now that, we don't know," he countered teasingly. "Just because planet Earth didn't have the technology back then doesn't mean another solar system did not."

Hannah shook her head and stepped back, but let him continue to block the wind for her. "Ooh." She lifted her hands and facetiously wiggled all of her fingers. "Spooky."

"Course—" Joe made a show of rubbing his jaw "—the lights could be poltergeists."

She tilted her head, not sure whether he was pulling her leg or not. She studied him with a smile. "You really think so?"

"All I know is that when they appeared just now and I saw them for the first time, I got chills down my spine."

So had Hannah.

"Which would explain why, reportedly, sometimes the lights are really playful, and dance around and bob all over. And other times, they apparently come down from the sky really slowly, and then seem to land, before taking off again at warp-speed and—"

Joe stopped in mid-sentence and stared.

Hannah turned and looked in that direction, too. Her voice caught as she watched, mesmerized, as a dazzling display of colored lights bounced all over the place. Before their eyes, the lights began fading then turned white-yellow, then blue, then red and orange again. "Are you seeing what I'm seeing?" she asked hoarsely.

"Oh, yeah." Joe pulled her close again. Standing slightly behind her, one arm around her shoulder, the other at her waist. "Even if that is a laser light show put on by some jokester or festival organizer."

"I know," Hannah agreed with a smile. "Wow."

They stood, snuggled together, watching the mysterious lights in silence for the next few minutes. Until finally, the sky went dark once again.

They could hear the murmur of disappointment ripple through the people gathered over at the viewing station.

"Think it will happen again?" Joe asked.

"Honestly?" Hannah shrugged. "Probably not."

He grinned. "Well, it was amazing while it lasted."

"So what do you really think is behind the phenomenon?" She asked him, as they turned to face each other once again.

Joe clasped Hannah's hand and held tight. "I don't think it really matters when it brings people together this way," he said softly.

Hannah couldn't agree more.

BY THE TIME THEY DROVE into Marfa and checked into the hotel it was late. Hannah waited in the Land Rover with Isabella while Joe set up the playpen, then she carried her sleeping daughter inside. She gently lowered Isabella onto the mattress of the mesh-sided crib and covered her with a blanket.

Joe left and returned with their luggage, being careful not to disturb the sleeping baby, too.

While he went about unpacking his own bag, Hannah slipped into the bathroom. Instead of changing into her pajamas, she sat down on the edge of the tub, and wondered why it was she was about to go to bed alone while on a weekend getaway with the man she wanted more than anything. She thought about the moral support and companionship he had provided since the day they had left for Taiwan. She recalled the tenderness he had shown her and her baby, the fierce passion that had led them to make love…and the rationale behind their decision to remain just friends. She sighed over the fun they'd had this evening and the fact that he was leaving in a few days. And then suddenly, she knew what she had to do.

She opened the door again. Still dressed.

Joe crossed the darkened hotel room and stood in front of her. "Everything okay?"

Hannah grabbed hold of his shirtfront. "It will be." Her decision not to waste another second of another day propelling her, she drew him inside the bathroom and shut the door behind her.

He looked at her expression and knew. A ragged breath escaped his lungs. "Hannah…"

The whisper of her name was so soft, so sexy. She clung to him and pressed her face into the hollow of his shoulder. "I know what we said. That we wouldn't…" A frustrated sigh escaped her lips. The truth was she had never been more aware of a man in her life. The warmth of his skin, the latent strength in his touch…the inherent kindness in his eyes… "But I can't stay away from you. Not when we have so little time left together."

Joe groaned. He drew his hands through her hair. Brushed his thumbs across the curve of her lips. "I don't want to stay away from you, either." His mouth covered hers, warm and insistent. His hands slid down her back, to cup her buttocks and lift her against him. He kissed her again, the force of it slamming through her like the downward thrill of a roller coaster ride.

"You understand," Joe said, his voice sounding strangely unsteady, "this doesn't change anything."

Hannah shut her eyes against the harsh reality of the bathroom light and luxuriated in the feel of his desire, pressing into her. "I know." But truth be told, their lovemaking changed everything for her. Making love with Joe made her feel loved. It made her feel as if once in her life she had everything she had ever wanted, everything she had ever needed. It made her feel as if so much was possible.

It didn't matter it wasn't going to last.

What mattered, she decided, was that she had the memories that could last her a lifetime. Would *have* to last her a lifetime.

JOE HADN'T EXPECTED TO have Hannah in his arms again. Now that she was here, he didn't want to ever let her go. That emotion carried over in his kiss, in the way he touched her, held her, in the way he lifted her onto the counter and made love to her there. And in the shower…and in the bed. Until finally they were wrapped together, holding each other as tightly as they had latched on to this moment in time.

"Joe…?" her voice whispered in his ear.

Joe gathered Hannah closer yet. He reveled in the sating feel of her skin and hair. He pressed a kiss to her temple, still holding her tightly. "I don't want this to end, either," he told her gruffly.

And maybe, he thought with new abandon, it shouldn't. Maybe they shouldn't just end it now but instead should give it time, see what happened, see if she would continue to want him in her life as desperately as he was beginning to want her—and Isabella—in his.

He drew back, not sure he was everything she needed in a lifelong mate, but willing to try. "We haven't talked about a long-term affair."

The smile curving her moist lips lit her eyes. "The kind that spans decades," Hannah asserted dreamily.

Relief flowed through him. They were on the same page after all. He breathed in the intoxicating womanly fragrance of her, kissed her cheek, then her lips. "It would work for me," he promised.

She cuddled closer. "For me, too," she purred, content.

"THAT MUST HAVE BEEN some festival," Valerie remarked, when Joe and Hannah walked in with Isabella just in time for the Callahans' annual picnic on Labor Day. "'Cause the two of you sure look happy."

Hannah felt happy. Maybe because what had started as a brief fling had turned into so much more…

Valerie stopped what she was doing, as the next thought occurred to her. "Wait. Does this mean I don't get the cabin?" she asked anxiously, setting down the vegetable tray she was about to carry out to the backyard, where the party was going on.

Joe blinked. "Why wouldn't you be able to rent the cabin?"

"Because," Valerie retorted as if he was the biggest idiot in the world, "you decided to stay."

Hannah plucked a cracker off another tray. Surprised at how serene she felt, she settled Isabella in her high chair. "Joe isn't staying, Valerie. He's leaving tomorrow for Big Bend, as planned."

Ruthann looked up from the tray she was preparing, in that instant reminding Hannah so much of her late mother. "Then how can you look like you just won the lottery?" she asked, confused.

Hannah got out two jars of baby food and thought about how to frame her answer. Finally, she just smiled and said, "Because we're officially 'an item.'"

"An item," Gus repeated, scowling, as he came in the back door. He turned to Joe. "I'd like a word with you, fella. In private."

Chapter Fourteen

For lack of a better place, Gus and Joe stepped into the garage. "What in tarnation do you think you're doing, stringing my daughter along like that?" Gus demanded.

Aware this was some kind of familial test—one he was determined to pass with flying colors—Joe looked Gus right in the eye. "I'm not stringing her along."

"Then what would you call it?" Gus barked.

"Look, Gus, I know you mean well here, but Hannah is a grown woman with a mind of her own. She doesn't need your protection." *Especially not from me...*

Gus's eyebrows shot up. "If my daughter agreed to be your woman whenever it's convenient for you and at no other time then I disagree."

Joe's patience began to fade. "Hannah knew from the outset what kind of work I do."

Gus stabbed the air between them with his index finger. "And you've known where her responsibilities lie."

Joe knew he had nothing to apologize for. "I've never asked her to leave the Mercantile or you."

Gus scowled and shook his head in obvious regret. "I thought you were an honorable man. I thought when the time came you'd change your mind and stay. Obviously, that's not going to happen." Disgusted, he turned away.

Joe waited until he looked at him again before continuing to explain the reason behind his actions. "I have a book to finish. Another to write. Research to do in Australia."

"And where does that leave my daughter and granddaughter?" Gus cut in, even more emotionally. "Hannah and Isabella deserve more than just the occasional visit from you. They deserve someone who is going to stick around!"

The guilt Joe had been holding back, flowed freely within him. "Hannah knows what I can offer," he insisted.

Gus scoffed. "And she says it's enough?"

Joe thought about the acceptance in Hannah's eyes and the warmth in her kiss. "Yes."

Gus folded his good arm beneath the arm in a cast and sling. "Then she's lying to herself, because no one who values family as much as Hannah does is going to be content with a romantic relationship that is run like a revolving door."

"Dad!" Hannah's cry echoed in the silence of the garage.

Gus turned. "Go back inside, Hannah."

"No, I will not." She closed the door behind her and marched toward them, hands balled into fists at her sides. She glared at Gus. "This is none of your business!"

"The hell it's not!" Gus countered, just as implacably. He held up a silencing palm before she could interject. "I admit, I haven't been there for you lately. Not the way you deserved, and not the way you needed. But if you think I'm going to stand by and let this vagabond—with a hole in his chest where his heart should be—stomp all over you…"

"That's exactly what I expect." Hannah threw up her arms in frustration. "Not the stomping part. But the leaving it alone."

Gus turned to Joe. "You don't need me to tell you. You know what the right thing to do is."

Without another word, Gus left the garage, shutting the door behind him.

A short, awkward silence fell.

Hannah faced Joe. She was shaking she was so upset. "Forget everything my dad just said."

Joe wished like hell he could.

Unfortunately, it wasn't that easy. "I can't," he said.

"WHAT DO YOU MEAN YOU CAN'T?" Hannah demanded, her dreams of a happily ever after with Joe diminishing right before her eyes.

"Your dad is right," he said gruffly. He rested his hands on her shoulders and looked down at her. "The kind of life I can give you isn't going to be enough."

Aware this was turning into a nightmare, Hannah said in a thick voice, "I told you. I would be happy with whatever time we can steal for ourselves."

So what if neither of them had yet mentioned love?

She *felt* loved when she was with Joe.

And she knew, even though she hadn't said the words out loud, that she loved him, too, more than she had dreamed possible.

"Sure, now the setup would do." Joe stepped away from her, sounding a lot like her dad. "But what about a year or two or three from now? When you've seen me a total of twenty or thirty days out of the whole year? Then it may not seem so great, Hannah. In the meantime, as your dad would be quick to point out, time is passing. Isabella is getting older, and she's growing up without a dad."

Was he breaking up with her? Oh God, no… Hannah took

a deep breath and tried to remain calm. "She was always going to grow up without a dad, Joe. I adopted her as a single mother." Having Joe there had made the experience all the more perfect, but it wasn't required. She still knew in her soul that she could bring up Isabella on her own and do a fine job of it.

Regret darkened his green eyes. "The thing is, Hannah, it doesn't have to be that way," he countered. "You can still get married. Have all the things you dreamed about as a little girl."

Exasperation warred with the deep disappointment welling up inside her. He was ending it. Damn it! "You don't know what I dreamed about as a little girl." Hannah spoke through her tears.

"Exactly." He swallowed, looking as if he were in as much pain as she was. "And I probably never will because we'll never spend enough time with each other to find out these kinds of things."

Like he couldn't find a way to change that, too? Hannah shook her head, said hoarsely as the tears rolled down her face, "I can't believe you're going to listen to my dad and not me."

"I don't have a choice. Your dad is right. If we continue down this road, I'll only end up hurting you and Isabella in the end, and you have to know that's the last thing I want."

She resisted the urge to hurl something at him. "You're hurting me now!"

"Not as much as I will if we let this linger on." Joe held up his hands. "We have to face facts. I'm not the kind of guy who fits into a family."

She folded her arms across her chest. "You fit into mine just fine."

Joe's gaze narrowed. "Briefly, sure, but were I to keep seeing you between writing projects, this is exactly the kind of family turmoil you would face. Your dad would be pissed at both of us, only I'd get to walk away and you would still be here, taking the brunt of his disapproval. Just the way you did before, when you decided to adopt Isabella over his objections."

"He came around. He loves her now. He knows I did the right thing. He'd eventually feel the same way about you, Joe."

Joe shoved his hands in the front pockets of his pants. "No, he won't, because he's always going to think I'm shortchanging you and Isabella and he is going to be right. And the hell of it is, you and I both know—over time—you are going to come to the very same conclusion."

Hannah swallowed, the pain in his voice mirroring the anguish in her heart. "No, I won't. Joe." She trembled, then forced herself to say, "I love you."

His eyes glimmered. "And I love you, more than I can say. Which is why," he finished in a low tortured voice, "we have to end this now."

Stunned, Hannah watched him open the garage door and walk away.

She knew, even before he got in his SUV that he meant what he said. He wasn't coming back.

THREE DAYS LATER, GUS CAME into the Mercantile just after closing and approached the coffee and ice-cream soda bar. "How long are you going to stay mad at me?" he asked.

Hannah shrugged and looked over at Isabella, who was happily strapped into a high chair at the end of the bar, chewing on a teething biscuit. "Does it really matter?"

Gus sat down on one of the leather and bronze stools next to his granddaughter. He smiled fondly at Isabella, who returned his adoring glance. Then he turned back to Hannah, his countenance surprisingly pleasant. "I'll have a chocolate soda, please. And of course it matters," he continued, lifting his gnarled hand expressively. "I don't think we should go through life not speaking to each other."

"Well, I don't, either," Hannah replied. She opened up the glass over the freezer compartment. "But I also know we have an example to set and until I can think of something pleasant for us to converse about…" She let her voice trail off as she added a scoop of chocolate ice cream into the tall glass, squirted in soda and added a dash of whipped cream. A few chocolate shavings, a maraschino cherry and a straw completed the treat. She wiped her hands on a towel and slid the glass toward her father.

"How about we start with how wrong I was telling you not to adopt a baby?"

Hannah felt a lump in her throat.

"Because I was wrong about that, you know." Gus leaned over and pressed a kiss on the top of Isabella's head. "This little girl is the light of your life—and mine. And frankly—" he paused to kiss her tenderly again "—I don't know what we would do without her."

Tears formed in Hannah's eyes. She swiped at them with the back of her hand.

"And I want you to know," he continued evenly, looking Hannah straight in the eye, "that I could not love her more if I tried. And I'm glad you went halfway around the world to get her. Because the thought of her, without a real home…well, it bothers me, that's all."

Hannah's lower lip quavered. "It bothers me, too."

"Then we agree. You did a good thing. And Isabella is a wonderful addition to our family."

Her dad's soda looked so good, Hannah decided to fix herself one, too.

"As for Joe…" Gus continued.

"I don't want to talk about him," Hannah said stubbornly.

"I do."

"Dad…"

He held up a palm. "I know you want me to say I was wrong, interfering the way I did."

"You were wrong," Hannah interrupted, deciding she didn't want a soda after all.

"No. I wasn't. You need more than a boyfriend who comes around every once in a while."

As much as Hannah was loathe to admit it, she was beginning to realize her father was correct about that much. She already missed Joe so much. The thought of him being gone for weeks and months at a time, over and over again, was almost more than she could bear. Or would have been able to bear, she amended silently, had the two of them still been together.

"What I don't follow is why you are so willing to sell yourself short in this regard." He searched her face. "You've never had a problem going after what you want in business. You tell it like it is, say what you want and go after it, no holds barred. Yet in your relationship with Joe, and to some extent I must admit reluctantly, with me, you dance around what you want. Refusing to put it all on the line."

"Well, maybe that's because—" she began.

"I haven't always been the easiest person to talk to?" Gus ventured.

Hannah shrugged. She walked around the bar to sit on the stool next to her dad. "We always had Mom to act as interpreter between us before. When I couldn't make you understand," Hannah confessed, "she could."

"And now she's gone."

Hannah nodded, new tears rolling down her cheeks.

It was Gus's turn to swipe at his cheek with the back of his hand. "I miss her, too, honey. More than I can say. But I also know she would want us to talk with each other like this, even when we don't agree. She'd want you to make me understand, whatever it takes, however long it takes. And she would want you to do the same with Joe."

Hannah's breath hitched in her chest.

"Did you or did you not want to marry Joe?"

Hannah did her best to pull herself together. "Of course, under optimum circumstances, that would have been nice," she said through her tears.

Gus studied her over the rim of his soda. "Did you ever tell him that?"

She felt herself getting defensive again. "I knew what the deal was when I got involved with him, Dad."

"So in other words you never asked for what you wanted."

No, she hadn't, and she regretted that more than she could say. She looked away. "I wasn't going to put him on the spot."

"Why not?"

Hannah turned back to her father, needing him to understand this much. "It wouldn't have been fair."

"Was the way it was going fair to you?" he challenged.

A silence fell, almost as painful as her breakup with Joe.

Gus stood and hugged her as best he could, given his arm was still in a cast and a sling. "I didn't raise a quitter, Hannah. If Joe is what you want, if you need Joe to make you happy, then stop feeling sorry for yourself. And do something about it."

"YOU KNOW," VALERIE SAID to Joe when she caught up with him in the dining room of the historic Gage Hotel. "I thought I was stupid for getting involved with Chris Elliott but I've got nothing on you."

Joe put down his dinner menu. So much for capping off three long days researching Big Bend National Park with a nice meal. Solo, of course. He arched an unwelcoming brow as he watched his cousin pull up a chair. "Aren't you supposed to be at work?"

Ignoring his lack of manners, she regarded him with a shake of her head. "I arranged to take off however long I needed to track you down."

"Hannah knows you're here? She said you could do this?"

Valerie looked at him as if he were a complete dunce. "Of course I didn't tell Hannah what I was up to! I told Ruthann and Marcy. They're covering for me while I help out 'a friend in need.'"

"We're family."

"As well as friends. And besides," Valerie pointed out, grinning impishly, "if I'd said *family*, it would have given it away."

"Not necessarily," he said, wondering where the heck the waiter was. "You have other relatives."

Valerie smiled. "None in as much of a crisis as you."

Joe swore silently. "I'm not in a crisis."

She shot him a look as if she begged to disagree.

"I imagine you didn't tell Gus where you were headed, either," Joe inquired.

Valerie accepted a menu from the waiter. "I didn't want to upset him."

"If that's the case, then you shouldn't be trying to get me and Hannah back together because that will definitely not put Gus in high spirits," Joe said.

Valerie scowled. "Gus will be in a good mood when you come to your senses and make Hannah and Isabella as happy as they deserve to be."

Her observation sent a flicker of hope soaring through Joe. "They're unhappy?" He did his best to play it cool.

Valerie scoffed. "What? Did you think they'd have a parade? Of course they're unhappy! Hannah's so sad it breaks my heart—although she puts on a good front when she's around the baby—but the truth of the matter is that Hannah hasn't stopped hoping you will come back." She glared at her cousin. "Every time the phone rings or someone comes to the house, she lights up. And then when she realizes it's not you, the joy is sapped right out of her. You can just see her spirits deflate. Look, Joe, I may not have ever been in love myself—in retrospect I see it was just an infatuation I felt for Chris Elliott—but I know it when I see it. Hannah loves you as much as you love her. And don't get me started on how much Isabella adores you!"

Joe was unable to deny any of that. He hadn't denied it to Hannah, either. "Unfortunately, that doesn't mean I'm the kind of man Hannah needs," he said sadly.

"Give me a break, coz. You're miserable, too!"

Joe exhaled. He wished the situation were different. He wished he were different. "I'm doing what's right for everyone in the long run."

Valerie shook her head. "What would be right is you rejoining the family, Joe. And whether you realize it or not—Hannah, Gus, Ruthann and Isabella are as much your family now as I am."

AT NOON THE NEXT DAY, Joe had finally marked everything off his to-do list and was ready to check out when a knock sounded on his hotel room door. Irritated by anything that was going to delay what he needed to do next, he strode to the door and opened it. Hannah stood on the threshold, looking incredibly lovely in the same white dress she had worn the day she first met her daughter.

She had a manuscript in her hand, a determined look on her face. "I finally got around to proofreading those pages of yours," she told him nervously. "You'll be happy to know I only found a couple of errors."

Joe took the manuscript and put it aside. "That's great."

Was that the only reason she had come? Hoping like hell it hadn't just been for closure, he ushered her in.

"And I want to apologize for taking so long to read them." Hannah turned toward him in a drift of rosewood and patchouli perfume. "I think, subconsciously, that I thought maybe if I never actually got around to reading them," she confessed wryly, "that you would never actually leave Summit."

He knew he'd been wrong to abandon her the way he had. "Obviously, that wasn't true," he admitted regretfully, ready to do penance for that and so much more.

She took a deep breath and let it out. "A lot of things we were thinking weren't true," she said quietly, taking him into her arms. "Like we could make love without falling in love."

Joe stroked a hand through her hair. "And I do love you," he said, kissing her tenderly.

"As much as I love you." Hannah returned his kiss with abandon, then paused to look deep into his eyes. "The real question is, what are we going to do about it?"

Joe smiled. "Obviously, from the way you're looking at me, you have an answer…."

She nodded. "I do." She encircled her arms about his neck and held him even closer. "I think you should marry me."

He didn't know whether to laugh at the irony of the situation or shout with joy. "You're proposing," he repeated, wanting to make sure they were very clear about their intentions this time.

"I am." Hannah held him all the tighter. "A very wise man—who in this case happens to be my father—told me not to be afraid to tell a man what I want and need. And what I want and need is to be your wife, and have you as my lawfully wedded husband."

Joe regarded her with all the tenderness he possessed. "Put that way," he said softly, kissing her again, "how could I say no?"

Hannah kissed him back, just as joyfully. "That's a serious yes?"

"Serious," Joe confirmed, reaching into his pocket, "as in this ring." He presented her with a sparkling platinum diamond ring, and said hoarsely, "I finished up here early so I could drive back to Summit and ask you to marry me at sunset. But, seeing as you've already asked and I've already said yes, then we'll just put on the ring." He slid it on her finger, then paused to indulge in another lengthy kiss.

When at last they broke apart, Hannah said, "About your work. I know you still have to travel."

"Not like before. I talked to my publisher this morning. The Australia project is going to another writer. I'm going to be doing a book on Arizona, and then another on how to travel the Gulf Coast." Deciding he didn't need to check out so quickly after all, he danced her backward toward the bed, sat down and pulled her onto his lap. "I'll still have to check places out, in person, but they'll be short trips, and if we work it out, you and Isabella can go with me."

Hannah traced his jaw with her thumb. "You don't mind?"

He shook his head. "I've spent the last thirteen years traveling the world alone. It's time I came home to stay, time I had a family of my own." He kept his gaze on her face. "So what do you think? Is November too soon for a wedding?"

THE SUN INCHED HIGHER in a cloudless blue sky. Hannah stood on the porch of her childhood home, breathing in the crisp autumn air. Her father walked out to join her. He was dressed in his Sunday best.

He paused to smile at the child clasped in Hannah's arms, then bent to kiss Isabella's forehead. Smiling, Gus wrapped his arm around Hannah's shoulders and bussed her cheek. "In case no one's told you, you two ladies look absolutely beautiful today."

"You look mighty fine today yourself."

He winked with the good cheer he had exhibited every day since she had become engaged. "Not every day I get to walk my daughter down the aisle," he quipped.

Hannah gave her dad a hug. "Speaking of which… Do you think it's time we headed for the church?"

Gus embraced Isabella, too. "I'm ready if you are."

Hannah buckled her daughter into her safety seat and climbed behind the wheel, while her father rode in the passenger seat. As she drove, she thought about how much her life had changed since August.

She had settled into the role of Mommy more easily than she ever could have imagined. Isabella went to the store with her every morning, and napped at the house every afternoon while Hannah took care of Mercantile business in her new home office. Meanwhile, Joe wrote, and her father—who was learning to cook as one of his new hobbies—figured out what they were going to have for dinner.

The new Web site was a success, as was the computerized inventory and accounting system. Locals and tourists alike loved the new coffee and ice-cream soda bar, as well as the retooled look of the place, and sales at the Mercantile had taken off once again. Gus had been so pleased he had permanently handed over the running of the store to Hannah. When he wasn't helping out around the house or doing rehabilitative physical therapy for his arm and shoulder, he could usually be found one of two places—either with his much loved granddaughter or Ruthann.

Isabella was thriving under all the attention. Hannah felt very much at peace. Joe seemed equally happy. He had whittled his travel down to two research-packed days a week, and for the first time in his life couldn't wait to get home to family.

The only glitch in that had been Valerie's continued feud with her parents. But at least she was going back to college for the spring and summer semesters to finish her degree. She was excited about it, too, providing she still had her job as assistant manager at the Mercantile upon her graduation.

Hannah had been happy to agree.

She and Joe were adopting a baby brother for Isabella the following August, from Taipei. Having Valerie on board permanently would mean Hannah'd be able to cut back on her own hours to spend time with her family.

And of course it helped, Hannah thought, happily, that Gus had become something of a father figure to Joe's cousin, as well. For the first time in her life, Hannah felt like she had a sister. And soon, a husband, too, she thought, parking behind the chapel.

Inside, all was nearly ready.

Valerie took charge of getting Isabella into the white lace dress she was going to wear during the ceremony. Ruthann helped Hannah slip into her off-the-shoulder ivory satin wedding gown.

In lieu of a veil, Hannah was wearing a wreath of flowers in her hair, identical to the one her mother had worn when she married Hannah's dad. Isabella had a wreath pinned into her hair, too.

Soon, it was time.

Hannah walked down the aisle on her father's arm.

Joe stood next to the minister, looking resplendent in his tuxedo, Isabella clasped in his strong arms. Both were smiling as Hannah reached them, and Gus gave her away.

With Isabella settled in the front pew on her grandfather's lap, Joe and Hannah turned to each other.

"I, Hannah, take thee, Joe, to be my lawful wedded husband..."

"I, Joe, promise to love and cherish you, Hannah...and love and protect Isabella...from this day forward..."

"Joe, you may kiss your bride," the minister said.

And Joe did.

* * * * *

*Cathy Gillen Thacker continues
her MADE IN TEXAS: FAMILIES OF THE
LONE STAR STATE series
with THE INHERITED TWINS,
coming October 2008,
only from Harlequin American Romance!*

*Ladies, start your engines with a sneak preview
of Harlequin's officially licensed
NASCAR® romance series.*

Life in a famous racing family comes at a price

All his life Larry Grosso has lived in the shadow of his
well-known racing family—but it's now time for him to
take what he wants. And on top of that list is Crystal
Hayes—breathtaking, sweet…and twenty-two years
younger. But their age difference is creating animosity
within their families, and suddenly their romance is the
talk of the entire NASCAR circuit!

Turn the page for a sneak preview of
OVERHEATED
by Barbara Dunlop
On sale July 29 wherever books are sold.

Rufus, as Crystal Hayes had decided to call the black Lab, slept soundly on the soft seat even as she maneuvered the Softco truck in front of the Dean Grosso garage. Engines fired through the open bay doors, compressors clacked and impact tools whined as the teams tweaked their race cars in preparation for qualifying at the third race in Charlotte.

As always when she visited the garage area, Crystal experienced a vicarious thrill, watching the technicians' meticulous, last-minute preparations. As the daughter of a machinist, she understood the difference a fraction of a degree or a thousandth of an inch could make in the performance of a race car.

She muscled the driver's door shut behind her and waved hello to a couple of familiar crew members in their white-and-pale-blue jump suits. Then she rounded the back of the truck and rolled up the door. Inside, five boxes were marked Cargill Motors.

One of them was big and heavy, and it had slid forward a few feet, probably when she'd braked to make the narrow parking lot entrance. So she pushed up the sleeves of her canary-yellow T-shirt, then stretched forward to reach the box. A couple of catcalls came her way as her faded blue jeans tightened across her rear end. But she knew they were good-natured, and she simply ignored them.

She dragged the box toward her over the gritty metal floor.

"Let me give you a hand with that," a deep, melodious voice rumbled in her ear.

"I can manage," she responded crisply, not wanting to engage with any of the catcallers.

Here in the garage, the last thing she needed was one of the guys treating her as if she was something other than, well, one of the guys.

She'd learned long ago there was something about her that made men toss out pickup lines like parade candy. And she'd been around race crews long enough to know she needed to behave like a buddy, not a potential date.

She piled the smaller boxes on top of the large one.

"It looks heavy," said the voice.

"I'm tough," she assured him as she scooped the pile into her arms.

He didn't move away, so she turned her head to subject him to a *back off* stare. But she found herself staring into a compelling pair of green...no, brown...no, hazel eyes. She did a double take as they seemed to twinkle, multicolored, under the garage lights.

The man insistently held out his hands for the boxes. There was a dignity in his tone and little crinkles around his eyes that hinted at wisdom. There wasn't a single sign of flirtation in his expression, but Crystal was still cautious.

"You know I'm being paid to move this, right?" she asked him.

"That doesn't mean I can't be a gentleman."

Somebody whistled from a workbench. "Go, Professor Larry."

The man named Larry tossed a "Back off" over his shoulder. Then he turned to Crystal. "Sorry about that."

"Are you for real?" she asked, growing uncomfortable with the attention they were drawing. The last thing she needed was some latter-day Sir Galahad defending her honor at the track.

He quirked a dark eyebrow in a question.

"I mean," she elaborated, "you don't need to worry. I've been fending off the wolves since I was seventeen."

"Doesn't make it right," he countered, attempting to lift the boxes from her hands.

She jerked back. "You're not making it any easier."

He frowned.

"You carry this box, and they start thinking of me as a girl."

Professor Larry dipped his gaze to take in the curves of her figure. "Hate to tell you this," he said, a little twinkle coming into those multifaceted eyes.

Something about his look made her shiver inside. It was a ridiculous reaction. Guys had given her the once-over a million times. She'd learned long ago to ignore it.

"Odds are," Larry continued, a teasing drawl in his tone, "they already have."

She turned pointedly away, boxes in hand as she marched across the floor. She could feel him watching her from behind.

* * * * *

*Crystal Hayes could do without her looks,
men obsessed with her looks, and guys who think
they're God's gift to the ladies.
Would Larry be the one guy who could blow all
of Crystal's preconceptions away?
Look for OVERHEATED
by Barbara Dunlop.
On sale July 29, 2008.*

HARLEQUIN

///// NASCAR

Ladies, start your engines!

Pulse-accelerating dramas centered around four NASCAR families and the racing season that will test them all!

///// NASCAR

OVERHEATED
Barbara Dunlop

Crystal Hayes could do without her looks, men obsessed with her looks and guys who think they're God's gift to the ladies. She'd rather be behind the wheel of a truck than navigating cheesy pickup lines. But when Crystal runs into Larry Grosso at a NASCAR event, she meets the one guy who could blow all her preconceptions away!

Look for
OVERHEATED
by Barbara Dunlop.

Available August wherever you buy books.

Feel the RUSH on and off the track.
Visit www.GetYourHeartRacing.com for all the latest details.

Harlequin® Historical
Historical Romantic Adventure!

From *USA TODAY*
bestselling author
Margaret Moore

A LOVER'S KISS

A Frenchwoman in London,
Juliette Bergerine is unexpectedly
thrown together in hiding with
Sir Douglas Drury. As lust and
desire give way to deeper emotions,
how will Juliette react on discovering
that her brother was murdered—
by Drury!

*Available September
wherever you buy books.*

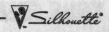

SPECIAL EDITION

A late-night walk on the beach resulted
in Trevor Marlowe's heroic rescue of a
drowning woman. He took the amnesia
victim in and dubbed her Venus, for the
goddess who'd emerged from the sea.
It looked as if she might be his goddess of
love, too…until her former fiancé showed
up on Trevor's doorstep.

Don't miss

THE BRIDE WITH NO NAME

by *USA TODAY* bestselling author
MARIE FERRARELLA

*Available August
wherever you buy books.*

REQUEST YOUR FREE BOOKS!
2 FREE NOVELS PLUS 2
FREE GIFTS!

Heart, Home & Happiness!

YES! Please send me 2 FREE Harlequin American Romance® novels and my 2 FREE gifts (gifts are worth about $10). After receiving them, if I don't wish to receive any more books, I can return the shipping statement marked "cancel." If I don't cancel, I will receive 4 brand-new novels every month and be billed just $4.24 per book in the U.S. or $4.99 per book in Canada, plus 25¢ shipping and handling per book and applicable taxes, if any*. That's a savings of close to 15% off the cover price! I understand that accepting the 2 free books and gifts places me under no obligation to buy anything. I can always return a shipment and cancel at any time. Even if I never buy another book from Harlequin, the two free books and gifts are mine to keep forever.

154 HDN EEZK 354 HDN EEZV

Name _____ (PLEASE PRINT) _____

Address _____ Apt. # _____

City _____ State/Prov. _____ Zip/Postal Code _____

Signature (if under 18, a parent or guardian must sign)

Mail to the **Harlequin Reader Service:**
IN U.S.A.: P.O. Box 1867, Buffalo, NY 14240-1867
IN CANADA: P.O. Box 609, Fort Erie, Ontario L2A 5X3

Not valid to current subscribers of Harlequin American Romance books.

Want to try two free books from another line?
Call 1-800-873-8635 or visit www.morefreebooks.com.

* Terms and prices subject to change without notice. N.Y. residents add applicable sales tax. Canadian residents will be charged applicable provincial taxes and GST. Offer not valid in Quebec. This offer is limited to one order per household. All orders subject to approval. Credit or debit balances in a customer's account(s) may be offset by any other outstanding balance owed by or to the customer. Please allow 4 to 6 weeks for delivery. Offer available while quantities last.

Your Privacy: Harlequin is committed to protecting your privacy. Our Privacy Policy is available online at www.eHarlequin.com or upon request from the Reader Service. From time to time we make our lists of customers available to reputable third parties who may have a product or service of interest to you. If you would prefer we not share your name and address, please check here. ☐

HAR08R

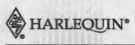

HARLEQUIN®

American ★ Romance®

CATHY McDAVID
Cowboy Dad

THE STATE OF PARENTHOOD

Natalie Forrester's job at Bear Creek Ranch
is to make everyone welcome, which is an
easy task when it comes to Aaron Reyes—the
unwelcome cowboy and part-owner. His
tenderness toward Natalie's infant daughter
melts the single mother's heart. What's not
so easy to accept is that falling for him means
giving up her job, her family and the only
home she's ever known....

***Available August
wherever books are sold.***

LOVE, HOME & HAPPINESS

www.eHarlequin.com   HAR75225

Romantic
SUSPENSE

**Sparked by Danger,
Fueled by Passion.**

Cindy Dees
Killer Affair

Seduction in the sand…and a killer on the beach.

Can-do girl Madeline Crummby is off to a remote
Fijian island to review an exclusive resort, and she hires
Tom Laruso, a burned-out bodyguard, to fly her there
in spite of an approaching hurricane. When their plane
crashes, they are trapped on an island with a serial killer
who stalks overaffectionate couples. When their false
attempts to lure out the killer turn all too real, Tom and
Madeline must risk their lives and their hearts….

**Look for the third installment
of this thrilling miniseries,
available August 2008
wherever books are sold.**